MINNIE'S R
THE PEACETIME
MOLLIE PANTER-DOWNES

Persephone Book Nº34
Published by Persephone Books Ltd 2002
Reprinted 2008 and 2020

These stories originally appeared in *The New Yorker*

© 2002 The Estate of Mollie Panter-Downes

Endpapers taken from a furnishing fabric
purchased from John Lewis in the late 1950s,
in a private collection.

Typeset in ITC Baskerville by Keystroke,
Jacaranda Lodge, Wolverhampton

Printed and bound in Germany
by GGP Media GmbH, Poessneck

ISBN 978-1-903155-24-0

Persephone Books Ltd
59 Lamb's Conduit Street
London WC1N 3NB
020 7242 9292

www.persephonebooks.co.uk

MINNIE'S ROOM:
THE PEACETIME STORIES OF
MOLLIE PANTER-DOWNES

PERSEPHONE BOOKS
LONDON

PUBLISHER'S NOTE

Many of the readers of the stories in *Minnie's Room* will already have read *Good Evening, Mrs Craven*: The Wartime Stories of Mollie Panter-Downes, published by Persephone Books three years ago. The Afterword, by Gregory LeStage, outlined the circumstances in which they were written: that Mollie Panter-Downes started writing for *The New Yorker* in 1938, when she was thirty-two, went on until 1984, and during these (nearly) fifty years published an extraordinary 852 pieces for *The New Yorker* and for no-one else. 'The range of her contributions is as impressive as the sum. It includes poems, London Letters, book reviews, Profiles, Letters from England, Far Flung Correspondent pieces, Reporter at Large coverage, Onward and Upward with the Arts columns, numerous one-off articles – and thirty-six short stories.'

Mollie Panter-Downes had begun writing when she was sixteen: *The Shoreless Sea* (1923) was a hugely successful novel which made an impact similar to that of Françoise Sagan's *Bonjour Tristesse* in the 1950s. Three more followed, *The Chase* (1925), *Storm Bird* (1930) and *My Husband Simon* (1931). None were reviewed quite as rapturously as the first although all were respectably received. She also wrote short stories for magazines and then, with admirable self-confidence, suggested to her agent that she should try and write something for *The New Yorker*. The idea was dismissed, but Mollie persisted, sending them a poem and a piece about Jewish refugee children arriving in London in 1938. Very soon she was writing short stories for them, and by 1940 was included in an anthology of *New Yorker* writers. After that not a year would go by until she was over eighty without *The New Yorker* publishing something by her, and sometimes a great deal.

Between the outbreak of war in 1939 and the end of 1944 she wrote twenty-one short stories, but none during 1945 – possibly the news coming out of Germany put a stop to any thoughts of the light-hearted, the comic, the ironic, even the descriptive. Then, during the early summer of 1946, she began the novel which forms a kind of backcloth to her subsequent writing: it is on the one hand a culmination of the wartime short stories and on the other anticipates those to come. *One Fine Day* (at first called 'The Vanished House') is an elegiac description of England just after the war and an intimation of its future. 'Sharply observed, witty and beautifully written, it is an English classic' commented a recent dictionary of twentieth-century writers.

'Miss Panter-Downes is concerned with the social and moral decline of the middle classes' wrote the *Times Literary Supplement* when *One Fine Day* was published in 1947. In fact the people she describes, struggling to adapt to their new circumstances in an England changed irrecoverably by the war, are determined that their decline shall not be moral whatever other changes they are forced to make: 'Wretched

victims of their class, they still had dinner' she wrote about Laura and Stephen in *One Fine Day*. But Stephen changes his outlook:

> And it suddenly struck him as preposterous how dependent he and his class had been on the anonymous caps and aprons who lived out of sight and worked the strings. All his life he had expected to find doors opened if he rang, to wake up to the soft rattle of curtain rings being drawn back, to find the fires bright and the coffee smoking hot every morning as though household spirits had been working while he slept. And now the strings had been dropped, they all lay helpless as abandoned marionettes with nobody to twitch them.

His mother-in-law, however, remains fossilised:

> The war had flowed past her like a dark, strong river, never pulling her into its currents, simply washing to her feet the minor debris of evacuees, food shortages or worry over Laura. Now, said Mrs Herriot, thank God it was over, and everything could get back to normal again. . . . So the mahogany continued to reflect the silver polo cups pleasantly, the Herriot world held together for a little longer in its deadness of glacial chintz strewn with violets and side tables strewn with the drooping moustached faces of yesteryear. The war had been horrible, really ghastly. . . . But mercifully it was over, said Mrs Herriot, and Laura must really pay

attention to her appearance a little more now that Stephen was home.

When, immediately after finishing *One Fine Day*, Mollie Panter-Downes wrote the first of her post-war short stories, she continued to explore this theme of the English middle class struggling to try and live in the same way that it had enjoyed before the war. The family in the title story are unable to believe that their maid wants to leave them to go and live in a room of her own. An elderly couple emigrates to South Africa because of 'the dragon . . . out to . . . gobble their modest, honourable incomes' (50,000 people went there in the 1950s). The brothers and sisters in 'Beside the Still Waters' grumble because 'Everything is so terribly difficult nowadays. [We] seem to be slaving . . . trying to keep the place going.' Many of the stories are about people who once had glorious lives, either because they were more affluent or because they were powerful in India or simply because they had once been young and were now old. In every case they are images of a once-great past now brought low.

Britain may have won the war but peace was disconcertingly grim. The late 1940s were 'The Age of Austerity', a drab time when a range of wartime controls and restrictions were still in place: for example, bread was *newly* rationed in 1946 and clothes were strictly utility; the government had incurred enormous liabilities to pay for the war and the country had to 'Export or Die'. By 1947 the spirit of wartime unity had faded away and life was not much fun for anyone. The year began with the worst weather Britain could

remember, and coal ran out; by the summer there was a severe balance of payments crisis and emergency measures were taken; and in August the Raj came to an end and a nation that had formerly ruled over an Empire finally had to accept that its decline had begun.

Yet despite the restrictions and crises (the economist Keynes talked about a 'financial Dunkirk') the Labour Government was seeking to build its 'New Jerusalem': in a few short months it laid the foundations for the Welfare State, set up the National Health Service and brought coal, electricity, gas, and railways into public ownership. But the essential background to the stories in *Minnie's Room* is that it was the middle classes that were enormously and disproportionately hit by the huge burden of Income Tax necessary to accomplish these changes. In 1935 it had been 4s 6d in the pound i.e. 22.5%; during the war it rose to 10s i.e. 50%; but then, in 1945, it was kept at 9s in the pound – far, far higher than ever before in peacetime. The country was dependent on the middle classes paying taxes almost at wartime rates; but as a result they suffered a dramatic change in their standard of living that was widely and deeply resented.

The stories in *Minnie's Room* are acute descriptions of a class and a nation in decline. But although they are socially observant, perceptive about emotions and accurate about the details of everyday life – they are nevertheless fiction. This was something about which *The New Yorker* was never entirely convinced. In 1952 their libel lawyer pointed out that in 'What are the Wild Waves Saying?' 'you might perhaps have gone to a little hotel like Mrs Marlbury's in your childhood

and might have reproduced details about it that would make the place identifiable – details like the elephants and other India touches in the lounge, for instance – and that you might have based your portrait of Mrs Marlbury on a real hotel keeper. If it is identifiable, he says the libelled people would be Mrs Marlbury and the vet and the sea captain.' And so on for a page and a half. Mollie Panter-Downes replied that 'Mrs Marlbury is a mixture of people I have known, and none of the originals were hotel keepers. The episode itself was, in fact, suggested by a real life experience, but not in those surroundings at all, or in any of the supposed circumstances.'

Her response was as restrained as her work would lead one to expect, and indeed a recent *New Yorker* historian has singled her out as 'a writer whose grace and restraint mirrored her personality.' The stories in *Minnie's Room* have a subtle, very English depth of observation: they are revealing of their time but are also suggestive and funny, beautifully written explorations of the response to change, and of loneliness, loss and self-deception.

CONTENTS

MINNIE'S ROOM:
THE PEACETIME STORIES OF
MOLLIE PANTER-DOWNES

Selfishness of wealthy

MINNIE'S ROOM

16 August 1947

Minnie was an ugly little Londoner who had been cook to the Sothern family for twenty-five years. She had come to them 'just a raw girl', as Mrs Sothern was fond of explaining. The way she said it made Minnie sound like a lump of something dreadfully unappetising that Mrs Sothern's skill had converted into a masterpiece of a dish. The words seemed to imply that the Sothern ladies, between them, had taught Minnie everything she knew. The truth was that Minnie was that extremely rare thing among the English, a natural magnificent cook, who would have found her medium and her style whatever happened. Before the war, her dinners were memorable, and Mr Sothern would say to his wife that though Minnie's cooking was, of course, nothing like the French, when it came to something solid, like a roast bird or a perfect bit of salmon, you couldn't beat the English. He was a big man, leaning, with Minnie's assistance, toward corpulence. All the Sotherns were substantially built, and their house in Bayswater was veiled with muffling plush curtains and full of large, softly curved objects filled with down, covered with rosy glazed chintz, or padded with leather. Even the china figures in the drawing-room cabinets contributed to the overstuffed effect, representing, as they did, bonny, plump shepherdesses and well-fed sheep. When you entered the front door and planted your feet on the thick Turkey carpet, you breathed comfortable virtues in the air along with a whiff of whatever delicious food Minnie was cooking.

Since the war, the Sotherns had visibly shrunk. The ruddy skin of Mr Sothern's face began to hang loosely here and there, like a too large overcoat worn by too small a man. Mrs Sothern was the only member of the family who was still stout – stouter, if anything – for she had developed heart trouble and was an invalid. Her daughter, Norah, did everything – changed the library books, stood in the queues, and exercised the cairn terrier in Kensington Gardens. In the old days, City friends of Norah's brother, Maurice, had sometimes looked at his sister thoughtfully as they leaned back after one of Minnie's excellent dinners and accepted a cigar from the old man. But now her big-boned figure had a settled, spinsterish look as she came back from her walks through the leafy squares, the little dog at her heels, to the Sothern house, which had escaped the bombing but looked somehow deflated, shabbier, like its owners. When she turned the key in the lock and opened the front door, the cairn ran in happily, knowing no comparisons, feeling no difference in the air as he trotted upstairs and jumped up on the faded glazed roses at Mrs Sothern's feet.

One day in May, when the square was alight with lilac and laburnum, the little dog trotted upstairs as usual and bounded to his place on the sofa, but the expected caress did not come. Surprised, he turned his little brindled snout toward the more expressive end of Mrs Sothern, who, taking no notice of him, flung out her hand toward Norah, entering with the shopping basket.

'One might as well talk to a stone!' she cried.

Norah set down her basket. 'You've spoken to her, then?' she said.

'Spoken!' Mrs Sothern's plump, ringed hand pawed the air, and emotion worked her flushed face. 'My dear girl, I've been practically on my knees. I put everything up to her – my health, the way you have to slave already, the fondness we all have for her. "Mr Sothern is devoted to you, Minnie," I said.'

'She seems to have made her mind up, all right,' Norah said, calmly enough. She lit a cigarette. There's nothing for it now, she thought, but to close this place and go to live in a hotel. But it will kill them, she thought. Mother will be lost without her big bedroom, with its familiar mahogany bed, the family photographs in silver frames, the curtains blowing out toward the smell of lilac and the sound of a barrel organ playing in the square, and Dusty curled up in his basket by the brass fire-dogs. And poor Daddy, who likes the feeling that he can walk around the house blindfolded and lay his hand on his cigars, his boot trees, and his Dickens – how can he turn into one of the anonymous old men one sees uneasily drinking tea at little wicker tables in hotel lounges?

'Maurice must talk to her this evening,' Mrs Sothern was saying. 'She's always adored Maurice.'

'I don't think it will make any difference, somehow,' Norah said. 'After all, she always said this would happen, didn't she?'

'As though one ever took her seriously!' moaned her mother.

Minnie was leaving them. The unbelievable had happened. Her beautiful dinners were long ago a thing of the past, of course, but she was still an artist with what there was to cook. Mr Sothern sometimes observed that when one dined out in restaurants, everything tasted the same and one got up as hungry as one sat down, but at home Minnie managed to make food taste like food. Though the dry, red skin was loose now on Mr Sothern's jaw, he did well enough. The other maids had gone long since, and Minnie and Norah did the work between them. Everyone envied the Sotherns for having Minnie. She had her one little oddity, though, her harmless bee in the bonnet. She had often told Mrs Sothern that if she had not married by the time she was forty-five, she intended to leave private service and take a room of her own somewhere. The family had laughed occasionally about Minnie's room. 'Someone will marry her, confound him, for her apple pie alone,' Maurice had said lazily one Sunday lunch before the war as he poured cream over his second helping. But no man had asked for Minnie. Even during the war and the blackout, when London was full of lonely men thousands of miles from their women and looking hungrily for any waist to circle, any bosom to lean their heads against, Minnie had trotted home on her evenings out with no footsteps following, halting, and following hopefully again behind her. Fortunately for the Sotherns, no hint of her superb ability to keep a man's digestion tranquil and his temper perfect appeared in her tiny, sad marmoset's face. 'Poor Minnie, we are really her whole

world,' Mrs Sothern had said one day to her daughter, sighing with compunction as they paused and listened to the radio floating up from the basement, a vast, Victorian catacomb, in which the solitary Minnie seemed to rattle about.

However, only the night before this lilac-tossing, perfect May afternoon, Mrs Sothern's assumption proved to have been false. It was Minnie's birthday, her forty-fifth, and in the evening, after dinner, she came upstairs and tapped at the door of Mr Sothern's study, where he was sitting doing the *Times* crossword. It was for fear of upsetting Mrs Sothern's heart that she came to him first, Minnie explained. If it would suit them, she said, she would like to leave at the end of June, when the room for which she had spoken would be empty. She looked at him at one moment as though she were contemplating saying something about her feelings for his family and their long time together, but it was no good; she had no means of expressing herself except through those lyrical meals that she had been creating for them for twenty-five years. She withdrew to the catacomb. Forgetting Minnie's prudence, Mr Sothern charged upstairs to find his wife, who was already in bed. Norah came up; Maurice came down, attracted by the uproar, from talking to one of his friends on the extension telephone in his bedroom. He was still unmarried, and lived a life of which his family knew very little. 'Good Lord!' he said. 'So she really meant it!' Hard luck on the parents, he thought. He assumed immediately that, without Minnie, the house must go. He could dig in somewhere; only the other day Miles Carrington had asked him to share a flat with him. But what would the parents do? Hard luck on poor old Norah, too, he thought, looking at his sister's worried face and the grey in her hair under the electric light. She was tied to the old people forever; she hadn't a hope now. 'A room of her own!' Mr Sothern was saying angrily. 'Hasn't she a room here, perfectly decent and comfortable? She must have gone out of her mind!' Yes, wailed Mrs Sothern from the bed, Minnie was plainly demented. How could she keep herself on her own, for one thing? 'By daily cooking,' growled Mr Sothern, and there was a stricken silence. It was an unfurnished room, he added, in a district too far from Bayswater to make it even possible that Minnie would come to them by the day. She had been getting things together for it, piece by piece, for years, tucking away every penny and every present they had given her, cherishing every chipped and battered remnant of furniture that had been thrown out from the upstairs world and had found its way down to the basement.

In the middle of the confusion, Dusty began to scratch urgently on the door, as a signal that it was past his time for a stroll to the letter box. Rather glad to escape, Norah went down with him. As she passed through the hall, she heard Minnie's radio playing a dance tune, loud and gay. One knows nothing about anyone, thought Norah. It had been raining lightly. She stepped out into the twilight after the pattering small dog and strolled under the trees, enjoying the quiet and the smell of the damp earth beneath the lilac bushes after the agitated scene in her mother's bedroom.

It was the next morning that Mrs Sothern decided Maurice must talk to Minnie, but it made no difference, as

Norah had foreseen. He was perfectly amiable about 'having a try'. He lounged down to Minnie's quarters after dinner, which had been a melancholy meal, but he returned with scant comfort for the gloomy little party in the drawing room. Minnie had said, he reported, that she would be sorry to leave them indeed and that she realised what a fix she was putting them in, especially Miss Norah. 'Well?' said Mr Sothern impatiently. That, said Maurice, was exactly what he had asked. 'Well?' he had said to Minnie hopefully, and though he did not enlarge on this to his family, through his head had suddenly shot the possible explanation of her decision to leave them. By Jove, he had thought, has she got a man somewhere? It seemed incredible. She was such an ugly little devil. But nothing in that line, after all, should surprise one. He had amused himself with his idea as he sat there on the edge of the kitchen table, listening to Minnie's answer, which he later translated for the benefit of his relations. If a woman got to a certain age without finding a husband and kids, Minnie's philosophy stated, she ought to have something of her own, even if it were only one room that belonged to nobody else. She had made up her mind to it ever since she could remember. 'I wouldn't never respect myself again if I didn't stick to it, Mr Maurice,' she had said. He had nodded, still playing with the notion that it might be a man, after all. Though he knew it was really preposterous, it made him feel somehow warm and friendly toward Minnie, and his smile was almost knowing as he said, 'Well, good luck, whatever you decide,' and went upstairs again with his tidings to the desolate outpost in the drawing room.

The next few weeks were rather dreadful ones for the Sotherns. Norah, who had determined to keep the house going at any cost, visited employment agencies and explained the Sotherns' needs to unimpressed women presiding over dog-eared ledgers that had a disconcerting look of being theatrical props, full of false names. Mrs Sothern was more than usually querulous; nothing was right, and Norah's heart sank when she thought what it would be like after Minnie left. One day, at Minnie's invitation, she accompanied her to inspect the new room. It was at the top of a gaunt house on the south side of the river. Minnie proudly introduced Miss Sothern to the present tenant, a quavering old woman who was going to live with a newly widowed daughter in the suburbs. 'Oh, I suppose you would have thought it rather awful,' Norah said that evening to her mother, but she had been struck by Minnie's large and opulent air of showing her around a mansion. There was a big lime tree growing in the street, just opposite the window. 'In the hot weather, I shall get the smell lovely,' Minnie had said. Mrs Sothern brightened faintly for the first time after hearing Norah's description. How could anyone put up with one sordid room, she suggested, after having the run, more or less, of the Sotherns' large, comfortable house. Given a month or two, Minnie would certainly be back. Norah was silent.

The last dinner Minnie cooked for the Sotherns was a memorable meal, with every member of the family's pet weakness remembered. It had the awful solemnity of a final sacrament, and nobody could swallow it, though, as Maurice sensibly reflected, this was probably the last decent food they would see in the house for some time. He had made arrangements to live with a friend, so that it would be lighter for poor Norah, but he would be coming back two nights a week to see how the old people were getting on. During a particularly oppressive silence, he observed, 'After all, everybody's got the right to live the life they want to.'

'Damn it!' exploded Mr Sothern. 'We ought to be life enough for her! She oughtn't to need anything else.'

His words were the naked, shameless expression of what they were all secretly thinking, and they felt as though the master's goaded bellow had stripped them as bare as a party of Greek marble statues sitting around the mahogany board. They avoided each other's eyes. After the appalling meal was over, Norah slipped away to the kitchen. She had fetched from her room a small Sheffield tea caddy, which she had bought the day before in an antique shop near Paddington. It was to be her parting present to Minnie, who burst out crying when she received it.

'I'm going to miss you all terrible,' she said.

She dried her eyes and looked with pleasure at the little box, from which she promised to make tea for Norah any time Miss Sothern felt like taking the bus ride over. For a while, Minnie would not need to work, for she had saved up a bit. Norah could imagine her sitting in the summer twilights, the tea caddy beside her, looking out of the open window at the green cloud of the lime tree. The kitchen windows were open now, and people's footsteps echoed on the pavements as they passed the railings. Norah could see a woman's short, bare legs hurrying along, a man's longer stride keeping up

more leisurely. Minnie stood holding her tea caddy, facing Norah across the kitchen table.

'I'll be thinking of you all tomorrow evening,' she said.

For a moment, Norah had the most extraordinary emotion, a frightful pang of purest envy. She could hardly trust her voice to speak in its usual pleasant accents. As soon as she could finish with Minnie, she hurried from the kitchen. It was a warm evening, and the big, overcrowded house seemed very stuffy. Nostalgic Chopin sounded from the drawing room floor; Maurice played rather well. Mr Sothern, his back turned to the room, was staring gloomily out into the square. On her sofa, Mrs Sothern was going through the motions of setting out a game of Patience, but she dropped the cards as Norah entered.

'You've been talking to Minnie?' she said. 'Any hope, dear?'

Maurice stopped playing; Mr Sothern half turned his head, but only for a moment. Poor old Norah, thought Maurice, it's really hard luck. He returned to his Chopin, and the music continued for some time to sigh and murmur and ask the bewildered, plaintive questions they were all asking themselves, in their own ways, as dusk came in from the square, where the dusty lilacs were purple and white no longer.

miss places rather than people

THE EXILES

18 October 1947

At last, they made up their minds to it. They would go. It was a plunge at their time of life, as Arthur Stanbury said, but having decided to be bold, they set about it thoroughly and quickly. For months past, while they were still deliberating, they had had their names on the waiting list for a passage, and the final shove that pushed them over the brink of a decision was the fact that they had now been given a boat and a sailing date. They were, in black-and-white, Colonel and Mrs Arthur Stanbury, first-class passengers from England to Durban on a certain day. In no time at all, they had let their flat, tidied up their loose ends of business, and broken the news to their friends.

It was a wrench parting with the flat, on the fifth floor of a gloomy mansion block in Westminster, where the hall porter was an old soldier who had been in Arthur Stanbury's regiment and where their names had stood so long on the notice board in the entrance that the painted letters had begun to fade. Though the corridors were daunting to timorous visitors, the fifth floor was sunny and had, from some of its windows, a pleasant view of the river and the Houses of Parliament. Big Ben reminded the Stanburys a

dozen times a day how central they were, how delightfully at
the heart of London – near Arthur's club, near the National
Gallery (they were fond of pictures), and no distance at all
from Whitehall, where the Colonel often bumped into an old
crony heading for the War Office.

But now their home was theirs no longer. The new tenants
had already dropped in two or three times to ask apolo-
getically if they might take measurements of this and that
– a fella, a pleasant young fella (as the Colonel described
him later, with obvious loathing), and his painted-up pretty
little wife.

'Going to South Africa, I understand?' said the juvenile, a
harassed-looking civil servant of forty, as he crawled over the
drawing room floor with a tape measure. 'Ah, how I envy you,
sir! By Jove, Bunty,' he said to the wife, 'I think it will just take
it.' Take it? Take what, the Colonel wondered gloomily. He
could imagine the kind of furniture these two would bring,
the mess they would make of Violet's room. The little wife
smiled at him brightly as she stood there with her pencil and
notebook. 'Think of that sunshine!' she cried. She bent down
to her husband, and they murmured together of plugs for a
radio and the colour of a certain sofa, which, said the wife, she
'saw *there*' – and she pointed her pencil straight at the heart of
Arthur Stanbury's row of beloved first-edition Surtees. The
Colonel could stand it no longer. He fled. And soon after that
the men arrived to pull the Stanburys more completely, as
it were, apart – to crate up the Surtees, the silver cups the
Colonel had won at polo, the fine rugs, and the bits of his
mother's things from the old home in Somerset, all of which

later were to follow on, like faithful dogs tracking after the master and mistress, to the new house in the strange land.

The two Stanburys had varied slightly, their friends might have noticed, in the reasons they gave for the step they were taking. To his acquaintance at the club, Colonel Stanbury said that his wife, with her weak throat, could not possibly face another winter in England like the last. She was delicate, and their flat had been, all those coalless months, an Arctic hut, a polar waste, where you could almost see the icy breath settling on the silver cups and the crackling chintzes. When he spoke of the sunshine, the warm African sunshine, a sort of tremor would shake the grizzled heads and the copies of *The Times*. A sort of groaning sigh would travel around the circle of leather armchairs as their occupants looked out at Pall Mall in the rain, at the gap of the bombed building opposite, and at the shabby young women hurrying along the pavements with their bare, splashed legs nakedly twinkling under their mackintoshes. Violet could do some shopping in Durban, the Colonel would say – fit herself out from top to toe with thin clothes for the hot weather. And again the tremor would seem to shake the copies of *The Times*, as though the elderly men whose veined, brown hands grasped them, around whose clear blue eyes harsh Indian light and Egyptian noons and the long hours of watching on duck-shooting mornings had engraved innumerable little sharp lines and furrows – as though these men, the Colonel's friends and contemporaries, felt mournfully in their bones that the Gulf Stream of the good days was turned away from England's shores forever.

Violet Stanbury made no particular mention of her weak throat when she spoke to people of their departure. Arthur, she said, felt that Things were so bad that they must get out while there was still time. Arthur felt Things very keenly, she would say. As she spoke, Things seemed to assume the shape of a dragon that was now firmly couched in its lair beneath the hitherto benign towers of Westminster. This dragon, she implied, was out to devour the Stanburys and their kind, to gobble their modest, honourable incomes, to push them to the wall and bar every path with the lashings of its hideously powerful tail. In time, Arthur felt, the monster of Things would get the whole country down, and he did not want to be there to see the sorry business. Already he was sufficiently upset by it all, Mrs Stanbury said with a sigh. Maybe he was too old to adapt himself to the changes – or *they* were too old, as she loyally, not entirely truthfully, put it, for she was a gentle soul.

But Arthur had stalked around London, contemptuous and bitterly complaining, carrying his grumbles from the circle of leather armchairs facing Pall Mall to his wine merchant, from his bootmaker to Todhunter, the spectacled old man in Jermyn Street who had cut his hair for years and who could be trusted to say a few disgruntled words about Things before he had fairly tucked the towel around Colonel Stanbury's neck. There were no standards of craftsmanship today, the two of them would decide as Todhunter's scissors snipped away in the tiny old-fashioned shop while the people in the street passed and repassed behind the big green bottles of lotion and the shaving brushes that were displayed in the window. Look at this brush, now, Todhunter would say, fetching one to show the Colonel. Trash, at the price they were asking! In the old days, he wouldn't have had it in the place. And the dishonesty of everybody, not only artistically but actually. There was no honesty left in the people, there were no manners, there was nothing but this new, slipshod idea of working the shortest possible hours for the largest possible wage. Different in his young day, grunted old Todhunter, brushing the Colonel's erect back as he got up to go.

And, sure enough, bus conductors seemed to snap at Arthur Stanbury as soon as his cold blue eyes lighted upon them; he had only to put down a pair of pigskin gloves for a second on the seat of a railway carriage and they disappeared. His days were embittered with little insults, little pilferings, so that it really got almost to the point where he hated everybody and trusted nobody. It was then that Violet Stanbury began telling people that Durban seemed such an opportunity, with their nephew in South Africa, married and settled there for years, and only too anxious to make arrangements and pave the way for them.

'Having Walter and Eileen there will make all the difference,' she said on one occasion. 'And when we get settled in – Walter thinks there will be a chance of a house later on – and can have all our dear old things around us, it will really seem like home. I shall garden – I have always missed gardening, here in London – and Arthur will be able to ride again. We shall get so much *more* for our money, as Arthur says. And the climate is apparently quite ideal.'

With such soothing reflections, such cosily optimistic word pictures, she contrived to rattle along through the days that led the Stanburys to their departure. They said their good-byes, some painful. Chapman, the old hall porter, was almost touchingly upset at their going.

'When they drive a gentleman like the Colonel out of 'is own country, it's a sad business, and that's a fact,' he said frequently.

Chapman also believed in Things that were bad and would get worse and be the finish of them all. His one eye glared mournfully, the points of his smartly waxed, faded moustache stuck out as though they intended to testify to the merits of spit-and-polish right up to the end. He brought his married daughter and her little girl from Stepney to say goodbye to the Stanburys. Mrs Stanbury had always taken a friendly interest in the family. The little girl, Ivy, was sucking an orange as she stood staring around at the packing cases in the hall.

'Do you know, Ivy,' said Mrs Stanbury, 'Colonel Stanbury and I are going to live in the country where oranges come from.'

Ivy said nothing.

'Fancy that!' prompted her mother helpfully.

'Wouldn't you like to come, too, and be able to run out and pick an orange straight from the tree whenever you wanted one?' asked Mrs Stanbury.

'Naow,' said Ivy.

The child was unattractive, Violet Stanbury could not help thinking. But Arthur pursued the point with a strange ponderous playfulness.

'Oh, come!' he said. 'Wouldn't you like to go on a big boat, Ivy, and wake up one morning to find blue skies, sunshine, and no more dirty old London? How about that, eh?'

'Naow,' said Ivy.

Apologetic, Chapman shepherded his women to the door and dismissed the parade.

The worst farewells, strangely enough, were to places rather than to people. The Stanburys were getting on in years, after all, and it was quite possible that they would never see these curiously living bits of stone and mortar again, these streets and spires that suddenly had personalities more intense than those of their dearest friends. One day toward the end, they paid their last visit to the National Gallery, and afterward, without asking each other where they were going, found themselves trudging off arm in arm, as though instinctively, to the Abbey. It was a beautiful afternoon, and the great, blackened building looked like some strong old ship, sailing on its green lawns, removed from and alien to the little red buses and the tiny Londoners swirling about it. Inside, the shadows were full of whispers from the feet of the people who strolled along the aisles. The Stanburys, too, strolled and stopped and moved on again, under the marble stares of the dead statesmen and soldiers. The place, in this golden light, seemed to whisper with more than the echo of shuffling feet, with something far away, infinitely old, and yet so personal that Arthur Stanbury felt like answering, 'Yes?' He stood there, poker-straight and motionless, staring up at the soaring roof until his wife touched him on the arm and murmured that they must go.

On the way home, he said to her suddenly, 'Oh, by the way, Vi, I ordered *The Times* and one or two of the weeklies today.'

'Ordered *The Times*?' Mrs Stanbury repeated rather blankly.

'To be mailed to us, I mean, every day.'

'But won't there be good South African papers, dear?' she asked.

'No doubt,' he said. 'But one might as well keep in touch.'

'Of course,' she said.

'I dropped in at Todhunter's, too. He'll go on sending my special lotion, as usual.'

'I do hope it won't get broken on the way,' Mrs Stanbury said.

'No reason why it should if he packs it up carefully,' the Colonel said shortly.

That night, lying in bed, Violet Stanbury found herself listening to Big Ben's strokes with unusual attention. She was so used to them that they never kept her awake normally, but tonight, perhaps because she was overtired with packing and arranging, she seemed to lie waiting for every quarter hour. The familiar voice boomed out, heavy and imperturbable, as though it spoke for something that would outlast the Stanburys, outlast Things, outlast the lot of them. From the rigidity of Arthur's shoulder, just touching hers in the bed, she knew that he was also awake. All the same, she asked in a hushed murmur, 'Are you awake, dear?'

'Yes,' came his deep voice.

'Can't you sleep, either? How provoking! I suppose we're too strung up by everything.'

He gave a great sigh. They went on lying awake, stretched side by side, listening to the big clock measuring out, piece by piece, the time that was still left.

But at last there was no time left at all. They were in the taxi, driving to the station, having been shut in by Chapman with a final salute and a 'Good luck, Colonel!' His kind, ratty little face, genuinely moved, faded from their sight. Mrs Stanbury made a gallant attempt to laugh. She said waveringly to Arthur, 'Well, it's begun!' After that, they sat in silence, looking out at the heartlessly bright streets, the crowds hurrying along, so strangely indifferent, so preoccupied with their own business. The taxi was held up by a policeman who raised his arm to let a party of women, perhaps as many as twenty, cross the road. Violet Stanbury watched them with a curious intentness as they plunged across the taxi's path, clutching each other's arms, uttering loud screams of laughter and mock fright. They were mostly stout and middle-aged, and looked like charwomen, out together on some spree. Their hair was arranged in cast-iron waves and frizzy curls, as though newly released from the pins, and their jolly red faces shone as they shouted at the policeman.

'Ta-ta!' they yelled. 'Be good now!'

Grinning, he turned and waved the Stanburys' taxi on. The Cockney voices, still yelling 'Ta-ta!' as the driver grindingly shifted gears, seemed like the voice of London itself ironically speeding the travellers on their way. Quite suddenly, for the first time, Mrs Stanbury began to cry. The tears streamed down her face while she fumbled quietly for her handkerchief. She did not want Arthur to see such a ridiculous display, and she glanced at him furtively as she rummaged in her bag. The Colonel looked as though he were noticing nothing. He was sitting in his corner, bolt upright, arms folded, looking out at the street along which they were driving. His face was expressionless, but suddenly Mrs Stanbury noticed his forehead was wet, as though it were a very hot day. She stopped trying to find her handkerchief and took his hand.

And thus silently united, Colonel and Mrs Arthur Stanbury came at last to the place of their departure.

BESIDE THE STILL WATERS

30 October 1948

The taxi-driver cut straight down to the sea and along by the rain-swept promenade, where a few solitary walkers, manfully seeking health or laying up virtue in their own minds, butted, heads down, against the slanting wind, their raincoat collars turned up and their dogs scuttling, as though blown, across the glassy asphalt. Beyond them, the long strip of grey English Channel was dotted with specks of white foam that looked like thousands of paper sailboats uneasily rising and falling on the swell. When the taxi had drawn up outside the nursing home and Cynthia Dodd stood paying the driver, the wind blew so violently up the avenue that she was almost surprised to see the white curtains hanging decorously straight inside the windowpanes, instead of being twitched askew.

Clutching her hat, she struggled into the glass shelter of the porch, and instantly, while she rang the bell and smoothed her hair, she had a feeling that her brothers and her sister were there already. Their presence seemed to percolate through the black-painted wood of the door, with its brass nameplate. And, sure enough, when she was admitted to the hall, where the principal piece of furniture was a sagging sofa that had the air of having been curved out by the bodies of a succession of anxious people slumped down among its springs, there, on an arm of the sofa, were two masculine hats she recognised as her brothers'. With the extraordinary sense of character possessed by hats even when abandoned by their owners, the tweed hat shouted of Freddie, the black Homburg admitted discreetly to knowledge of Edward. Monica's headgear, if it had not accompanied its wearer into the matron's sitting room, would have been, in its mashed felt way, equally revealing.

Miss Halliday, the matron, appeared in a doorway. 'Ah, here is Miss Dodd!' she said brightly. 'Come right in – Major and Mr Dodd and your sister are waiting for you. What a terrible day! Not too wet, I hope?'

'No, thanks. I had a taxi from the station. Hello, Monica,' said Cynthia.

Her brothers and sister were gathered around the matron's gas fire. They greeted one another amiably but without enthusiasm. Meeting seldom, they generally parted as speedily as possible, and with a certain amount of relief. On such occasions, Cynthia found it difficult to think of herself and these three middle-aged adults as having at any time constituted a tight little unit known as a family, with a shared roof, habits, sentimental associations, and terms of reference. Like passports to prove that they had once had common nationality, they all had eyes of the same light, piercing blue – their father's eyes. But life had dealt so variously with this inheritance – in Edward's case blurring it with myopia, in Freddie's with fine red veins – that it no longer seemed to connect them.

It struck Cynthia that her relations and Miss Halliday welcomed her arrival as though hoping she would bring something to the situation that hung on the air of the neat and deadly room. Looking from one to another as she took off her gloves, Cynthia asked, 'How is Mother?'

'We're really very pleased with Mrs Dodd,' Miss Halliday said. 'Really *very* pleased. Dr Huggins will be along any minute now, and then he'll tell you the situation exactly. We felt that it would be best if we could get you all to run down for a little conference with us here on the spot.'

'Been telling Miss Halliday that it was a bit of a shock,' said Freddie. 'We thought that Mother was nicely fixed up here. Under Dr Huggins' eye, I mean, and all that.'

'If only she had our old home still, Miss Halliday, everything would be simple,' Monica said.

Monica looked warm and worried, thought Cynthia, as though she had literally run, as Miss Halliday phrased it, all the way from Hampshire, and was wondering who was going to give her husband and the girls their tea. Vestiges of everyone's interrupted everyday business seemed to have trailed into the room with them. Grasping handbags or gloves, they sat forward on their chairs like strangers brought together in a railway waiting room by some accident on the line.

'When do you want us to move her?' asked Cynthia, and Miss Halliday's eyeglasses flashed her an approving beam that said, At last, someone who talks business! Yes, I was right, this is the one to concentrate on. 'Naturally,' she said, 'we don't want to rush you, Miss Dodd. You'll want to make arrangements, I know.'

'I suppose there's no chance of a full recovery, is there?' asked Edward. 'No likelihood of a sudden improvement or, for that matter, any great change at all?'

'At Mrs Dodd's age –' Miss Halliday was beginning cautiously when the wind suddenly threw itself against the house, rattling the windows, and an electric bell rang sharply in the hall.

'That will be Dr Huggins,' said Miss Halliday. 'He'll explain everything you want to know, Mr Dodd. He has one patient to see before he comes in here, so if you'll excuse me for a few moments . . .'

Her exit seemed to make quite a stiff little breeze of its own.

'I call it really disgraceful,' Monica said indignantly, almost before the door had closed.

'No, I can see their point perfectly,' said Edward, taking off his glasses and wearily pinching the bridge of his nose. 'They're short of beds, and there are too many really ill people waiting for them. They won't keep old people like Mother, who have nothing particularly wrong with them except that they're old.'

'Mother has been *desperately* ill, Edward!' Monica cried.

'I know. But she's got over that amazingly well, and now there's nothing to do except – well, I suppose, to wait. They won't let her do that here. You can't blame them.'

'Would they take her back in her hotel, do you suppose, if we got a trained nurse?' asked Cynthia.

'I doubt it,' Edward said.

'My God, what a world for the old, eh?' said Freddie. 'Difficult to live and damned awkward to die, seems to me.

Better have something settled by the time Huggins comes down, hadn't we?'

'I'd love to have Mother,' Monica said rapidly, 'but I don't at the moment see how I could. I haven't got a soul to help me, and I don't think George would let me try and cope with any more. Besides that, now that Janet is home, there isn't an inch of spare room. Of course, Mary could turn out and go into the little sort of attic with Nannie, and the nurse could – but, even so, it wouldn't work. It's a hopeless house to have an invalid in.'

'I'd say it was a good deal better than my place,' said Freddie. 'We've got a couple of land girls living in, and it's cold as the devil, too. I can't get the coal to heat it for more than a couple of months. Marjorie had one go of flu after another last winter.'

'At least you have plenty of milk, which is more than we have in Hampstead,' said Edward.

Freddie nodded grudgingly.

'I'm afraid I can't say a thing,' Cynthia said. 'You know the size of my flat. Cigarette, Edward?'

'Thanks, no. Of course you're out of the question with only one room,' said Edward irritably.

'I don't really see why Nannie couldn't look after Mother perfectly well without a nurse,' said Monica. 'She's with her most of the time here, as far as I can see.'

'Probably she could,' Freddie said. 'Huggins will be able to tell us that. But who's going to have them? That's the question.'

'We'd practically fixed up to let a fellow called Yates, in the B.B.C., have half the house,' said Edward. 'He isn't the noisy type, and it helps nowadays, I don't need to tell you. We can put him off, of course. Nothing has really been settled.'

The others looked at him uneasily.

'Old people must be kept warm,' said Freddie. 'That's the trouble. If things were normal, I wouldn't hesitate.'

'I know what you mean, Freddie,' Monica said. Her face was flushed. 'Everything is so terribly difficult nowadays. George and I seem to be slaving every minute of the day trying to keep the place more or less going. It sounds ridiculous to say that I can't take on any more, but I don't believe I could.'

There was a gloomy silence. Cynthia said abruptly, 'I think I'll go up and see Mother now. There may not be time after we talk to Dr Huggins.' She glanced at her watch. 'I want to catch the four-ten back to London.'

'That's the one I'm trying for,' Edward said. 'I've got a meeting this evening. Yes, you go on up, Cynthia. Monica and I saw her for a moment before you came.'

'I'll come, too,' Freddie said. 'It might be better to hear what Huggins says before we decide.'

The light from a Victorian stained-glass window on a landing scattered ruddy warmth on Freddie's tweeds and slightly drooping cheeks, so that he looked auburn and mournfully doggy, with his red-rimmed little eyes, as he growled, 'These places! Hope Marjorie has me put down before I ever land up in one of 'em.' In the passage of closed doors, behind which there were separate exhausted silences, a vase of mauve carnations and a tray on which stood a glass and a plate of fruit rinds were like footprints in the soft mud beside some vast, silent river, proving that life still existed there.

'Wiltshire is damp in the autumn,' said Freddie. 'I'm sure Huggins will say so. Is it Number Fifteen? When I was down last . . .'

They found Nannie, their old nurse, who had stayed on as maid to Mrs Dodd, sitting by the window, getting the light for a bit of sewing.

'I thought you'd be up,' she said, taking off her glasses and putting her finger to her lips. 'She's asleep now. It tired her seeing the others.'

She drew back the screen from the bed.

'Don't wake her,' Cynthia whispered.

Mrs Dodd lay on her back, with her hands folded on her chest. Her face looked yellow between the two wisps of grey hair that Nannie had braided as she used to braid Monica's hair, tying the ends with ribbons. There was a bowl of fresh purple violets beside her, probably brought by Edward, a discriminating flower giver. The mantelpiece and bed table were crowded with family photographs, the usual selection, Cynthia noticed, arranged by Nannie in all the hotel rooms her mother had occupied since the house was sold, as though Nannie insisted on uniting the family in double leather frames, however carefully they avoided each other in the flesh. Here the pictures were again, in the bleak nursing-home room – the faces of men and women, fat babies, loving dogs sitting panting into the camera, all of them saying that Mrs Dodd had existed. It was rather touching, Cynthia thought, the way poor old Nannie always trotted the entire gallery of pictures out and stuck them up as though they were something without which Mrs Dodd could not be decently seen, like her stays or her teeth.

'How is she?' asked Freddie in a hoarse whisper.

'Only fair, dear. Not much change. Sometimes she has worse days than others.'

Mrs Dodd's hands rose and fell on the polished skin of her chest. She had always been a stout, commanding woman, but now she looked strangely frail and refined, as though she had left all the attributes of the flesh outside the door of this room, as heaps of clothing are left by bathers on the shore.

'You know that they're turning her out, Nannie?' Freddie said, speaking louder.

'Oh, I know, dear. Oh, it's a regular shame. Such a worry to you all, I'm sure,' the old woman said trustingly.

Perhaps Freddie's voice had penetrated a little, for suddenly Mrs Dodd moved and, without opening her eyes, said in the unfamiliar voice her illness had left her with, 'Nannie?'

'Better go now,' Nannie whispered. 'I shan't say you were down, too. It might worry her.'

'Nannie?' the struggling voice asked again.

'All right, my duck, I'm here,' replied the old woman quickly, as Cynthia in her childhood had heard her answer a hundred times in the night. The voice stopped. Freddie closed the door softly.

They did not speak on the way downstairs. As they went into the matron's sitting room, they heard Edward saying cheer-

fully, 'I really think it might be the very thing,' and Dr Huggins saying, 'Well, I sent a case like your mother's to Mrs Draper's before. She used to be a nurse, you know, and now she takes just one or two elderly people into her home. Nothing very pretentious, but quite cosy – Oh, how do you do, Miss Dodd? How are you, Major Dodd?' he said as Cynthia and Freddie came in. He turned back to Edward. 'How about hopping into my car and going round right away to fix it up with Mrs Draper? She lives quite close.'

Monica stood up, buttoning her coat and picking up her bag, as though already heading thankfully for George and the girls. There was a faint congratulatory bustle in the room. And Cynthia found herself thinking with relief, too, of the train back to London, of the drawn curtains of her own room, with its walls too solidly built to feel the wind that blew here with such mournful, disturbing force off the sea. Nannie is the only decent one of the lot of us, the only one who will be there with love at the end, she thought bitterly, even while she stood listening to Edward explaining that Dr Huggins had come to the rescue with a really excellent suggestion.

I'LL BLOW YOUR HOUSE DOWN

25 March 1950

❖❖❖

The little girls, who slept in the old nursery next door, woke early, but their babbling did not wake their mother. Rhoda's morning sleep was heavy. Her room, which had been hers in her girlhood, showed neat and pretty in the cold light. The windows were open and the curtains twitched in the breeze. Beyond the lilacs and the prunus trees at the front of the house, a heavy truck rumbled along the country road, and Rhoda stirred slightly. Immediately, protestingly, she tried to tunnel back into the submarine dream meadows where Henry still walked and still had a voice. For a while after his sudden death, she had been able to imagine his voice constantly, saying all sorts of encouraging and tender things. Then, without warning, Henry had shut up. It seemed the final disloyalty that while he was so horribly, eerily dumb, his watch went on ticking merrily away on the table beside his widow. Surely it should have become dumb, too – its mechanism should have stopped when his did? Watches should sicken and die with their owners, like faithful hounds who grieve and stiffen on the door-sill.

In Rhoda's dreams, though, Henry was wonderfully there, and preoccupied with the things of this world. When the truck

31

had jerked her into semi-consciousness, he had just come bounding up a staircase she did not recognise, saying, 'Why must we ask the Fannings, of all people?' (Her dream memory refused to put any tender encouragement into Henry's mouth. The ringing, irritable voice from beyond the grave spoke always of tiresome acquaintances, lawnmowers, trains that did not go beyond Basingstoke, lost books, or torn overcoats.) But the truck had crashed too deeply into the delicate fabric of the dream for Rhoda to reply. Sadly she woke, staring up at the ceiling that had once seemed like the floor of heaven patined with bright gold and was now only the ceiling of her room in her parents' house, to which she had returned – Mrs Henry Baynes, with her two little girls.

She lay thinking of the day ahead. The noise in the nursery had been increasing, and now the door burst open and in rushed her children, half dressed. They were glowing with high spirits. One roof was as good as another to them, and they enjoyed living with their grandparents, who spoiled them. Rhoda smiled faintly at the sight of their pink faces and bobbing manes of sandy hair – Henry's colour, his authentic signature, his final and pathetic intimation of immortality. She stretched out an arm and caught at the younger child's little vest, asking, 'Do you know where I am going today?' But both children were screaming with laughter; they chased each other back into the nursery. There was no comfort to be had from them.

At breakfast, Rhoda's father asked her, from behind his paper, 'What time are you meeting these people?'

'The Dentons? Eleven o'clock.'

'Tell Wolfe that you ought to get them up a bit on five thousand pounds. After all, it's a very attractive little place.'

'I know, Father, but that's the best offer I've had. Mr Wolfe says the market is falling, and I think he's right.'

The children, pushing cereal into their rosy, milky mouths under the instructions of their grandmother, listened attentively.

'Mr Wolf, Mr Wolf!' one little girl chanted.

'Mr Wolf said to the little pigs, "I'll huff 'n I'll puff 'n I'll *blow* your house down!"' came with a rush from the other.

'Hush, pets,' their mother said.

'Well . . .' Rhoda's father folded his paper, pushed back his chair, and looked at his daughter as though he would like to say something helpful. Rhoda's widowhood embarrassed him. She had been such a pretty, lively girl, born to be happy, as they say, and now here she was, left alone and not too well off. He hesitated, gave it up, sighed, and escaped.

Later, when Rhoda went to catch the bus that would take her all the way to her and Henry's old home, her mother walked down to the gate with her.

'Are you quite sure that you wouldn't like me or Father to come, too, Rhoda?' she asked.

'Perfectly, dear, thanks.'

'Well . . .' Her mother sighed, looking helplessly around, as though anxious to take her mind from the thought of Rhoda coping with the sale of her home, of Henry dead.

The bus came at that moment, to both women's relief. Rhoda got in and settled down for the ten-mile journey. Ten miles, Henry had often said, was an excellent distance to be from even the most fondly loved parents – near enough for family meetings, far enough to discourage dropping in. Henry had hated to be dropped in on; he had deplored the impromptu in anything. The pretty home, so carefully planned, had provided for all eventualities except the incredible one of Henry's impromptu death. Now Rhoda could not afford to go on living there any longer. It was since she and the children had returned to her parents that Henry had suddenly withdrawn himself from her waking hours and had become mute, as though he no longer recognised Mrs Henry Baynes in the reinstated daughter of the house, sitting between the old couple at meals, going upstairs at night to the neat, virginal bower. After today, Rhoda thought, she would have finally severed all connection with her husband. She looked sadly out of the window of the bus at the familiar landmarks going by.

It was a bright March day. When Rhoda got off at the crossroads and walked up the lane, she could smell fresh spring smells rising from the damp bushes. She was not sorry to see Mr Wolfe's car standing at their gate. If she had arrived first, she would have taken a melancholy walk around the place, and would have made herself still more depressed. Mr Wolfe, cheerfully twirling keys attached to a label, appeared at the front door as she approached the house. He wore a public-school tie and had a breezy manner calculated to strike confidence in the breasts of hesitant clients.

'Ah, *there* you are, Mrs Baynes!' he said, as though reassuring her of her identity, her solid, fleshly manifestation there on the brick path between Henry's rose trees.

Smiling wanly, she felt quite glad to be reassured. This return – her first since the day she had moved out – was a bit ghostly. Before she could say anything, they heard another car coming up the lane, and Mr Wolfe, murmuring in her ear 'They're really very keen on the place – keen as mustard,' hurried down the path to meet his clients. Rhoda walked in, and stood waiting in the empty hall, where the silence from the rooms above, stripped of everything but dust and a few shavings from packing crates, seemed for a moment to be expectant.

Not for long, though. The presence of Mr and Mrs Denton, as they entered, immediately filled the house to overflowing, booming through its modest structure like strong sea echoes through a frail shell. They were a stout, elderly couple, so well padded with red and mauve flesh, with nappy dark cloth, with the handsome tanned skins of pig and calf and the narrow, shining brown pelts of small wild creatures from snowy forests, that tweedy Mr Wolfe appeared to be flattened between them like the filling of a thick sandwich. A small brindled dog had jumped out of the car after them and was sniffing the steps thoughtfully.

'Pleased to meet you, Mrs Baynes. We're glad you could come over this morning,' Mr Denton said hospitably, enfolding Rhoda's cold hand in a squeeze of expensive pigskin.

'Goodness knows why Mr Denton has taken such a fancy to the house,' Mrs Denton confided to Rhoda as they tramped upstairs, waking tremendous echoes. 'It's not really our style, though I grant it's quaint.'

'I'm buying it for the view,' Mr Denton said.

They were in Rhoda's bedroom. Mr Denton marched to the windows and waved possessively at the Hampshire countryside. 'The garden's not much, but come back in a year, Mrs Baynes, and I'll guarantee you won't recognise the place – inside or out. Look, Dolly, that chestnut will come down, for a start.'

Rhoda looked at him in horror. 'The chestnut? My husband and I were always particularly fond of it,' she said.

Mrs Baynes' widowed state flashed so plainly across Mr Denton's mind that he appeared to raise an invisible hat for a brief, respectful silence.

'Understand your feeling, naturally.' The hat was replaced. 'Makes for damp so near the house, though.'

To Rhoda, the room still seemed to be full of the shapes of familiar furniture. Standing right in the middle of Henry's bed, Mrs Denton explained, 'Mr Denton suffers from asthma.'

'Mr Denton!' cried Mr Wolfe reproachfully. 'This house is not *damp*, sir! You never found it anything but bone-dry, did you, Mrs Baynes?'

Busy with complicated emotions, Rhoda did not answer. Mr Denton, looking pleased, touched a wall with his gloved finger, and inspected the fingertip as though hopeful of finding it saturated.

In other parts of the house, Mr Denton waved his arms again, and other walls crashed, cupboards sprang up, new bathrooms blossomed. The air was so thick with spectral flying masonry that Rhoda felt inclined to jump back in alarm. Her home and Henry's was disintegrating under her eyes. In her imagination she could hear it groan, shudder, and fall apart. The rooms were very cold. Mr Wolfe's thin nose was pink above his drooping, tea-coloured moustaches, but his clients, bulky as polar bears, did not seem to feel chilly. Rhoda longed to be gone. While the others were discussing some electric fittings the Dentons wished to buy, she slipped away into the garden.

Standing quite still, with her back to the closed door, she drew a breath of relief. The garden, at any rate, still presented its familiar pattern, which she and Henry had planned. The daffodil and the tulip had outwitted the furniture vans; their green spikes were pushing up through the soil as if nothing had happened. An old wooden swing, not taken along when Rhoda moved out, hung from the chestnut tree. As she walked past, she gave it an absent-minded shove, and it began to creak backward and forward. The Dentons' dog, which she had forgotten, was sitting on the path beside their favourite seat, placed to command, through a gap Henry had cut in the trees, Mr Denton's prospective acquisition of Hampshire. Rhoda sat down on the seat next to him.

I shall go back and corner Mr Wolfe, she thought, and say that I have changed my mind. I cannot sell to those people. The trees, the grass, the white house at her back, all seemed to make their separate thin cries of protest at being abandoned to the Dentons. The polar bears were kind, no doubt, but she hated them. She closed her eyes and drooped her head, as though expecting to encounter a shoulder. Her sorrowing cheek, however, was pillowed only on air. Opening her eyes, she stared vaguely down at the Dentons' dog.

He was still planted in the same place, seeming to inspect the landscape, to sniff it with his little raised muzzle, which was peppered with grey hairs. He had grown old with the Dentons and would lay his bones somewhere here, near the stump of the chestnut tree. She went on looking at him, postponing the moment when she must go back to the others. He turned his head and regarded her with an air of deep melancholy. Behind them, not a sound came from the house. Mr Wolfe and the Dentons might, for all she knew or cared, have got into their cars and driven away.

It occurred to Rhoda that the dog was exactly as she had hoped that the unknown Dentons would be – grey, shadowy, fitting quietly into the picture without disturbing a single line. Only to such silent and tactful purchasers could she have handed over without a pang. The booming realities – the Dentons in the flesh, laying about them like house wreckers – were insufferable intruders. But she would sell to them all the same. She needed the money. She looked at their sad little dog, and she thought how he had spent all his life at the heels of the stout, furry creatures who were now waking the echoes somewhere out of earshot in her empty rooms. He sighed, the curiously resigned sigh of an old dog, and looked away. Did animals, she wondered with a touch of superstition that Henry would have deplored, perhaps understand better than humans? For in this companionable moment she arrived at a sort of truce of acceptance. Quite gently, she gave up.

'Mrs Baynes!' Mr Wolfe called from the back door.

Mr Wolfe drove Rhoda to his office, the Dentons following on behind in their car, to sign the necessary documents. Mr Denton and his Dolly had evidently compared notes on the way and were anxious to warm and cheer Mrs Baynes – to buck the poor little thing up, in short. After the business was over, they insisted on sherries in the crowded bar of the Red Cow, across the market place, and, drinking, seemed to wax larger and ruddier and to exude from their heavy, hairy wrappings some sort of exhalation, as though they were beasts softly steaming in the warmth of a byre.

By the time they were ready to leave, Rhoda had missed the bus, so Mr Wolfe drove her home.

'Between ourselves, Mrs Baynes,' he said, chatty with sherries, his eyes bright above the nipped nose and the pale orange-pekoe moustache, 'we did jolly well to get him up another five hundred quid. Choice little property, of course, in many ways, but not everyone's meat.'

'Their dog liked it,' Rhoda murmured.

Mr Wolfe gave her a startled glance. 'Oh, rather, yes,' he said heartily – he had probably misheard her. 'And Mr Denton being, I'm sure, the sort who will appreciate the place, he'll make a good job there. You'll see.'

Rhoda didn't reply that she would certainly not see. For the first time in months, outside her dreams, she had been able to hear Henry's voice, this time asking angrily why she had sold to the Dentons. They have a charming dog, she answered him. And suddenly, lightheaded in the rush of air after the sherry and the stuffiness in the pub, she wanted to laugh. Or perhaps she was lightheaded with relief that the dreaded business was over. She slipped lower in the seat, thinking drowsily how well and dreamlessly she would be able to sleep tonight. Yes, she thought, she would sleep like the dead.

- Family dynamics
- old people are a duty

THE OLD PEOPLE

5 August 1950

The Darlingtons had not been in the hotel a day before the other guests began to look at the younger Mr and Mrs Darlington queerly, with commiseration or veiled amusement or a touch of indignation, as though they had brought with them a large, unruly dog whose presence was likely to embarrass and upset the community. The eccentric member of their party was, of course, old Mr Darlington, who from the start had behaved as awfully as Cecily had predicted he would. As though her father-in-law were indeed a dog who was not house-trained and might disgrace them on the rug at any time, she said angrily to Lance when they met briefly in their room the day after their arrival, 'I told you what would happen! He's going to be impossible in a hotel. He'll make himself a nuisance to everybody, and probably break a leg, too.'

'Why should he break a leg more easily here than in Oxford?' Lance asked. He was hunting in a suitcase for his second pair of bathing trunks; the pair he had worn that morning was wet and he had promised to take the children swimming again before tea. The three of them, Julia, Frances, and little George, were waiting for him in the lounge.

Lance had appeared at breakfast that morning in shorts and an open-necked blue shirt, but the holiday garb sat on him strangely, with the look of a carefully planned fancy dress that would win its wearer a prize at a dance on board ship. His short legs, unveiled once a year, had a curious air of still being covered by a species of spiritual tweed. Although his clothes proclaimed him lounger, committed for two idle weeks to problems connected with prawning nets and thermos flasks, he looked too brisk to relax his real personality for an instant. Now, on his already inflamed face, his glasses made a tiny reservation of pale, town-dweller's skin from which his small, intelligent eyes looked out sharply. And sharply he said, 'I see no reason for such an unfortunate occurrence, dear.'

He had found the bathing trunks. He stood up, rolling them into a towel, and tucked the neat little package under his arm, where immediately it looked tamed and urban, like a book or a folder of papers.

'The stairs are very dangerous,' Cecily said. 'Your father has fallen twice already.'

'Against that we can balance the absence of under-graduates on bicycles,' Lance said as he started for the door.

'Your mother said he didn't sleep well last night, and you know what *that* means. I shudder to think what the people next door must have suffered.'

'Well, dear, the old people are here, and we must make the best of it. After all, we couldn't very well have abandoned them, could we?'

Cecily did not answer. Lance came back, slipped his hand under her chin, and kissed her good-humouredly. His kisses were apt to be literary. This one was, recognisably, a jolly buss, straight out of the Elizabethans. Then he went off to the beach with the children.

Lance's old parents had come to stay with him in Oxford after they sold their house, which had become too big and too difficult for the senior Mrs Darlington to manage any longer. They were trying to find a small flat in Oxford. Meanwhile, their presence made an uncomfortable squash for Lance, Cecily, and the children, especially during the holidays, when Julia and Frances were home from school. In the busy university household, the grandfather and grandmother sat about aimlessly. Cecily found them almost unbearable. Their room was a nostalgic junk heap of clocks, books, papers, felt slippers, tea caddies, medicine bottles, biscuit crumbs, and shawls, on which reposed the old man's Siamese cat, another and equally unwelcome émigré. The three visitors moped visibly, Mr Darlington missing his study, the Siamese his old scratching ground under the back-garden lilacs, and Mrs Darlington sighing as she sat and knitted socks for Lance. When the summer vacation for which Cecily had been praying arrived, Lance had insisted that it would do his parents good, take their minds off things, if they went along to the seashore, too. Under his hearty manner – all the little quips that put themselves sadly into quotes the moment he made them – he was stubborn and impossible to budge when he had decided on a course of action. So here they were at the hotel, the entire family, minus only the cat, over whose happiness Lance felt no filial qualms.

Mr Darlington was a big, shambling old man with a wild, scholarly head made more alarming by a tufty white beard. Inquisitive as a squirrel, he frightened the other guests considerably by opening their bedroom doors and peering in, then backing out again with a muttered 'Sorry, sorry.' And away he would go, plunging and stumbling down the passage with his curious walk, as though he had iron legs and were pitching forward toward an invisible precipice.

The hotel provided no private baths, so old Mr Darlington took his morning tubs in the bathroom nearest his room. He bathed slowly, a process accompanied by a seal-like grunting, loud, inexplicable crashes, and a heavy sloshing of water. Young Mr Kent, who sat with his bride at the next table to the Darlingtons' in the dining room, had only tried the bathroom door gently on the first morning when he was frozen in his tracks by a trembling roar from within: 'What is it? *Who* is it?'

Cecily had hurried out of her bedroom, opposite, and smiling charmingly, had said, 'My father-in-law won't be more than a minute or two now. I'm afraid he's rather slow.'

'Oh, it's quite –' Mr Kent had murmured, and through the door he'd called politely, 'Please don't hurry, sir. I'll go along to another bathroom.'

There was no answer – only some violent gargling – and the young man had fled.

Mealtimes, especially lunches and dinners, would have been extremely painful to Cecily if it had not been for Lance and the children. Lance talked incessantly, with the monotonous, grating sound of a piece of chalk moving over a blackboard, imparting a flow of information – local geological, botanical, and ornithological facts that he had imbibed before they'd been twenty-four hours in the place. With the uncontrollable habit of a lifetime, he reduced nature to an orderly card index. Most of his observations were addressed deferentially to his father, admiration of whom was another habit, which even the old man's senility could not break. Mr Darlington, although he was quite deaf, usually seemed to hear him and would nod, dribbling beer down his beard, and suddenly shout some question like 'See any gannets?'

A startled hush would then descend on the other tables, and the back of Mr Kent's neck turn red, and his young wife bow her head. Mostly, Mr Darlington muttered and attended to his food but every now and then, with the lack of control over the vocal organs shared by the deaf and the adolescent boy whose voice is changing, he boomed out a remark that sounded immediately as portentous and terrible as the utterance of a prophet. '*See any gannets?*' and thunderbolts were poised, the dining room quivered, and pretty Mrs Kent choked over a mouthful of food.

At breakfast, however, when the old gentleman was apt to be silent, the Darlingtons made quite a pleasant family picture – the old couple, the son and daughter-in-law, the children. Julia and Frances were strapping girls in their teens, and they kept up a cheerful babble. Little George took after his father; every subject was explored clearly and calmly to its furthest limit, and filed in the card index already maturing under his thatch of sandy hair.

'Stop talking and eat your fish,' Cecily would say to him.

'Eating their fish helps little boys to swim well,' old Mrs Darlington would probably add. At every meal the grandmother contributed the usual fond, tremulous whoppers, which George always considered for a long time, chewing slowly, before he finally gave the sceptical little cough like the one that preceded Lance's demolishing arguments. The likeness was really absurd.

Old Mr Darlington said almost nothing, merely sighing, slopping coffee into his mouth, and staring fixedly before him with his fierce faded-blue eyes while his wife made little dabs at him with her napkin.

'Oh, *look* what you are doing, Edward!' she would say. 'Oh dear, all down your tie! Oh dear, oh dear, what a pity!'

'And now, Mother, what would you like to do today?' Lance would ask punctiliously, as though he did not know.

The grandparents did not go down to the beach. They had tried that only once, on the first morning, a gusty day when the wind, blowing strongly off the Atlantic, shook their frail old bodies as if they were cutout paper figures. Lance had settled his mother on a campstool in the shelter of a rock, where she sat uncomfortably erect, her feet together, her gloved hands in her lap, and her hat perfectly straight on her white hair, as though she were paying a call in a vast, roaring, glistening drawing room. She looked a perfect mound of clothes – a thick little edifice of hairy cloth, scarves, watch chains, and strong shoe leather – among all the unclothed bodies lying on the sand at her feet.

Mr Darlington had gone careering off to the very edge of

the water, stumbling and pitching so perilously that Cecily thought he was going to fall in. But he had stopped in time, leaning on his stick and glaring out at the great green swells capped with white feathers. The waves seemed to spring hungrily toward him and then slink back again over the glittering sand, while their thunder filled the air. He had stayed there for some minutes, immovable. Then he came shambling back, sat down on a copy of *The Times*, and said not a word.

After that, Cecily had insisted that the old people would be happier in the hotel garden. On fine days Lance installed them there, near the tennis court, where the other guests skirted them warily, or, if the weather was dull, he left them indoors in the lounge, where they waited until he came to move them elsewhere. The beach and the sea were too big, too boisterous for them. And, Cecily bitterly commented, it made a break for the rest of the family to be without them for a few hours.

After a day or two in the sun, Lance's nose had begun to peel, so that he looked more than ever a professor in fancy dress, with a cardboard beak as the final carnival touch. He took all the most strenuous walks to the surrounding beauty spots, sometimes alone, sometimes accompanied by his daughters or the young Kents (usually a panting quarter of a mile in the rear). In no time at all, he had tidily filed away in his mind every notable view, church brass, and Celtic earthwork, and would shout a full description of them to Mr Darlington at dinner. Lance had taken a fancy to Mr and Mrs Kent. By the happiest chance, Mr Kent was flatteringly excited to learn who old Mr Darlington was – or, rather, had been, for it seemed impossible to reconcile the celebrated Oriental scholar with this restless, wispy ghost creaking and muttering around the hotel all day, and wandering around half the night with a flapping of slippers and a midnight rushing of toilet flushes.

'Why, I have his translation of early Chinese love lyrics,' little Mrs Kent had exclaimed to Lance, looking reverently at the old man hunched in his garden chair.

'What a magnificent head!' she'd said, and Lance, pleased, had begun to tell her about the Augustus John portrait of his father.

After that, the Kents must have spread the word around the hotel. To Cecily's relief, the other guests affected not to notice the old man's behaviour – distinguished old age was, after all, privileged – and they were brightly, tactfully blind when they caught Mr Darlington barging out of the wrong bedroom, or leaving the bathroom with his trousers erratically buttoned. Cecily sometimes noticed Mr Kent gazing at her father-in-law with romantic respect, as though he detected on the old man's food-spotted waistcoat a plaque that said, 'In this building, now ruined, Edward Munroe Darlington lived for many years.'

For their last afternoon, Cecily and the children had planned a picnic tea on the beach, but at the last moment Lance said they would have to go without him; he had decided to hire a taxi and take the old people for a drive.

'You know they're far better sitting quietly here in the lounge,' Cecily said.

'All the same, dear, I intend to take them,' Lance had

insisted. 'I want Father to see that very unusual inscription in the church at Mandeville Comfrey. I was telling him about it last night.'

Exasperated, Cecily cried, 'Really, what utter nonsense! You know very well that he takes in practically nothing now. It's an absolute waste of money and your last afternoon!'

Lance had finished collecting his usual equipment of compass, maps, and guidebooks. He did not stir anywhere without them, and was presumably prepared to pioneer his way back to Oxford if necessary. On a bench in the garden, Mr and Mrs Darlington were already waiting, staring patiently before them, coated and scarved, rugs over their laps. They resembled a couple of stoutly wrapped parcels put out on the steps for collection.

'We shall meet at dinner,' Lance said to Cecily, and departed.

As the party rolled off, Lance sitting facing the two inanimate parcels, his voice could be heard, like the voice of a guide in a tourist bus, raised in invincible explanations.

The others went down to the beach. Cecily lay in the sun while the children scrambled among the rocks. It seemed impossible that tomorrow they would all be back in Oxford. She would walk into the familiar hall; her brown hand, now curled indolently on the warm sand, would take the letters and telephone messages off the brass tray in its customary firm way. Everything would be as usual, including Lance's shrouded legs. The Siamese cat, with his peculiar melancholy cry, would dart out and wipe his head welcomingly against old Mr Darlington's baggy tweed trousers.

And once more, in fancy, Cecily could smell the curious stale, almost medicinal smell – the compounded whiff of cat and Petit-Beurre biscuits, of musty books and wintergreen, and the debris of two long lives laid up in mothballs – that would float out at her all winter whenever she passed the guest-room door. Mr Darlington's Siamese would be there to welcome him home. There was no doubt of that for Lance had said nothing of any change in plans. Cecily felt terribly depressed.

But the sound of the sea was soothing. The waves seemed like a voice, sighing on and on, endlessly repeating the same story, which rose to a climax, then subsided in a gentle, plaintive whisper. Cecily dozed off. When she woke, the children were chattering and splashing in the pools not far from where she lay. Drowsily, she listened to George's calm treble; he was dropping shells into his tin bucket.

'When I'm grown up, I shall live here always,' he said. 'I shall live here with all my children. We shall bathe four times a day, and *never* go to school.'

'Goodness!' Frances giggled in an elder-sister way. 'Will you ask us to stay with you, George?'

'No.'

'Little beast! Will you ask Mummy and Daddy?'

'No.' Cecily heard him drop some more shells carefully into the bucket – one, two, three, four. 'They'll be dead by then, I expect.'

Frances exploded with surprised laughter.

'George!' Julia, a serious girl, was shocked.

'Well, they will,' piped George, pleased with the sensation he had made.

'That's not funny, really,' Julia said. 'Let's go and bathe now. I'm roasting.'

Cecily lay for a few minutes longer, listening to the sea. The eternal story that it was sighing to itself was sad, after all, in its cadence of strong rise and dying fall. She had the impulse to do something vigorous and assertive to prove that she and Lance would be able somehow to change that ending, and she picked herself up and hurried after the children, calling to them to wait for her.

They were just capering into the sea, and they paused, turning their heads toward her.

'Don't go out too far!' she called.

To her own ears, as she stood on the wet sands and watched them nod and plunge away into the surf, her voice sounded thin and supplicating.

wedding couple ordinary after all but love made magical

WHAT ARE THE WILD WAVES SAYING?

3 May 1952

◆◆◇◆◆◇◆◆

Perhaps it was because of the little episode of Mr and Mrs Easton, which was one of those thunder-claps of experience that occur from time to time in life, that I remember Mackerel Bay very vividly. Otherwise, I might easily have blurred over mercifully in my mind that depressing stretch of English coast to which, as children, my cousins and I were sent year after year by our parents for the sake of the famous air. August after August, and occasionally, if the London winter had been particularly damp and foggy, for a fortnight in the spring as well, we were dispatched to gulp this celebrated, boisterous element into our lungs. When I went back to look at Mackerel Bay a short time ago, breaking a journey to turn off the main road and see if the place had altered since the old days, I found that the only thing completely unchanged there was the strong, salty wind, which still skittered among the dunes like a playful terrier, lifting the paper bags and the bathing towels of the picnic parties uncomfortably camped in the hollows of sharp grass, and nipping at the mottled legs of the children playing cricket on the sands against the cold-looking

53

sea. Everything else was much altered. The few lines of raw, red villas that even in our day had begun to change the appearance of the old fishing village had now multiplied into battalions, and shops and Moorish cinemas had sprung up along roads I remembered as sandy tracks where rabbits ambled and larks rose out of the gorse.

We children – my cousins Janet, William, and John, and I – were uncritically blind to Mackerel Bay's less attractive features, and we looked forward yearly to our return to Mrs Marlbury's private hotel, Sea View. I do not know where our family originally acquired Mrs Marlbury, but perhaps it was through friends of my mother's and father's, for Sea View offered tangible evidence that its owner, like my parents, had once lived in India. In the lounge, rows of small ebony elephants plodded doggedly, tusk to tail, in the general direction of the North Sea, and a huge, fretted brass gong glimmered behind the hissing bead curtains in the hall doorway. Three times daily the gong was pounded by Effie, one of the little maids, who appeared to have been crammed, breathless and about to burst, into their black stuff uniforms, shiny white collars and cuffs, and thick black stockings. In the conversation of Mrs Marlbury, a woman with a husky voice, which probably owed its fascinating furriness to the inevitable cigarette hanging from her lower lip, occasional Anglo-Indian words nested like exotic birds. Our elders disapproved of the cigarettes and of certain other aspects of Mrs Marlbury's personality, such as her friends the retired sea captain and the Mackerel Bay vet, who often called on her and stayed a long time shut up with her in the office, from which they would emerge, after much laughter and talk, looking rather flushed and sucking strong peppermints.

Whatever the relatives who shepherded our party to Sea View thought of Mrs Marlbury's friends, none of them could deny that the place was excellently run. My cousins and I thought Mrs Marlbury herself entirely satisfactory. Sometimes we speculated about the existence of Mr Marlbury, who seemed to have sunk without leaving a trace – not even an old hat on the hat-stand or a photograph in the office. Once in a way, Mrs Marlbury went up to London for a night or two on business, striding off, jaunty and blooming, in a tailored suit with a fur hanging down her back, its beady-eyed mask helplessly biting one of its tiny paws, like a hunting trophy dangling from the shoulders of a jolly, buskined Diana. Then it was easy to believe, as we all firmly believed, that the retired captain and the vet were passionate rivals for the hand of this dashing woman.

Aside from our family, Mrs Marlbury's most faithful visitors were an old couple called Rogers. August after August, we looked toward their corner table, as one turns to a certain wall where a familiar picture has hung since time immemorial, confident of finding them behind the tomato-ketchup bottle and the cruet, and there they always were, bowing and smiling their welcome. They were there every spring, too, drawn, like us, by the health Mackerel Bay was supposed to give in return for buffeting the breath out of your shrinking body. Mr Rogers was a retired manufacturer, and his little visits to Sea View were, I assume, a break in the idle tedium of life in the big industrial town where he had made his money and now had nothing to do but enjoy it. He and his wife were a very old, very dull couple. I am sure that they actually were old, unlike some other ancients out of my childhood, who, I have often realised later with a shock, could not have been a day over forty. Both the Rogers had white hair through which their pink scalps showed here and there, and Mrs Rogers' head nodded above the ketchup bottle, not only in welcome to the party of noisy children who were back again that year but perpetually, gently, as though in eternal agreement with some question that had been asked her and had left a bewildered expression in her faded blue eyes. She was very deaf, and her husband was very silent. My cousins and I found Mr Rogers a great bore, although he was always kind and would stop us as we trooped in to get tidy for lunch, piling our gritty sand shoes and buckets and shrimping nets in the glassed-in porch as we went through. He had been so busy all his life making money that the small change of light conversation had eluded him, and as he stood there, benignly beaming down at us and searching for something easy and jolly to say, inspiration never came. Instead, he would bend down and peer into one child's bucket and ask always the same question – 'Well, got any sharks in there?' We realised that this was meant to be humorous and generally managed a polite smile, but we dodged him as much as we could.

The old Rogers were a part of Mackerel Bay for us, as steady and dependable as the wink of the lighthouse in the evenings or the crouching shape of the curving headlands that enclosed the bay. Every morning they went out for a little

walk, and in the early evenings, after a nap in their room, they went out for another. We never saw them apart. In the teeth of the wind they toddled along, scarved and hatted and gloved as though still in the city, their arms linked tightly together. I wondered sometimes – when I saw them creeping across the sands or standing up on the higher ground where perhaps, if it were spring, they might have halted while Mr Rogers pointed with his stick toward a patch of primroses under a gorse bush – whether he supported his wife or she supported him on these outings. They walked cautiously and with a slight stagger, as though, thus joined together, they were competing in some extremely difficult three-legged race, the object of which was to deposit their old bodies at the goal of a sheltered nook of the dunes, or on a seat where they could rest and look out at the sea while they recharged themselves for the return journey. If the weather was too bad, they played Patience in the lounge.

One year, when we had gone to Sea View in April to clear up a winter of illness and had found the Rogers there, as usual, a more intriguing couple made a brief appearance in the hotel. My cousin Janet – she was fourteen, a year older than I was – spotted a scatter of confetti on the hall floor one afternoon as we came out of the dining room after high tea – a little spoor of shoddy-looking paper discs leading away into the darkness under the gong. Smartly clicking her tongue with annoyance, Mrs Marlbury swooped down and began gathering it up, bit by bit, explaining, 'Bride and bridegroom – fell out when he took his coat off, most likely.'

The information was thrilling to Janet and me, and I asked where the interesting pair were now. Mrs Marlbury's cigarette waggled up and down in a sort of contemptuous semaphore as she replied 'Gone out for a walk.' Taking the offending confetti into custody, she prepared to return to the office but stopped to look back at us. One eye executed a large wink, and the cigarette jiggled again as she delivered a last racy message. 'Spooning,' she said, and retired to converse with Mr Stemp, the vet, who had dropped in for his Saturday-evening visit. I could see him waiting in the office – a big man, reddish brown in colouring and clothing, and with distinct reminders of his trade in his long, hairy cheeks, his sad brown eyes, a certain porcine width and tilt to his big nostrils, and a dogginess in the way he looked at Mrs Marlbury.

A bride and bridegroom! The boys took the news coolly, but Janet and I could hardly wait to see the first honeymoon couple who had ever entered our lives. We were not, it seemed, a marrying family. Our younger aunts were unmarried, and an uncle who had taken an Australian wife had unsportingly gone through with the ceremony in Melbourne. But love had already loomed up in my thoughts and in my cousin's, encouraged by the surreptitious reading of romances, which always ended in tidy, blissful, and financially comfortable marriage. We knew that love was the unique experience of the brave and the fair, and, brooding over our own youth and physical shortcomings, we could only trust blindly in the miracle-working properties of time (again our reading provided comforting examples) to turn clumsy goslings into graceful swans. Now, we thought, we would see the romantic

fulfilment at close quarters. At Mackerel Bay, against that familiar backdrop of sea and sand and spiky grass all combed one way by the tugging wind along the humped spines of the dunes, a corner of the tremendous curtain was unexpectedly to be lifted before our eyes.

My first sight of Mr and Mrs Easton was the most appalling disappointment. They came into the lounge, where Janet and I were hanging about, pretending to be engrossed in books. The Rogers were playing Patience, Mrs Rogers' unsteady head seeming to express triumph as her freckled, thick-knuckled hand pounced here and there over the cards. Occasionally Mr Rogers tapped his finger on some card, to indicate something she was missing, and with a laugh she would put it right. I thought how deadly they looked, and how awful it must be to sit there playing the same old Patience evening after evening. Just then the door opened and a couple came in. At first I thought that someone else must have arrived at Sea View, and then, with a shock, I realised that they were the bridal pair.

The bridegroom was a weedy little man in a badly fitting tweed jacket. He looked as though he might be a clerk. He had rounded shoulders, a small, depressed moustache, and a townee's pallor. The bride was a spectacled, plain girl; her hard-looking newly waved hair had been loosened into wisps by the sea gusts, and she patted it self-consciously as she entered. She wore a tailored costume of a particularly hideous shade of puce, and her smile, as she answered old Mr Rogers' friendly greeting, was pleasant but toothy. The lovers sat down on a cane settee and regarded Mrs Marlbury's winding procession of elephants in silence. Janet and I looked at the pair in consternation.

Soon we escaped, to examine the shock. Up in our bedroom, which was as draughty as a gull's nest, and booming, like a hole in the rocks, with the thud and suck of the waves, we collapsed in laughter on the beds, where sand from our beach things had sifted a miniature Gobi over the India-cotton quilts. 'His boots!' moaned Janet. 'Her goggles!' I sobbed. But our laughter was hysterical, as though we had just been rescued unharmed from a collapsed house we had believed to be solid. We were dangerously shaken. I remembered with disgust the two ugly, insignificant people downstairs, who had broken my dream in which all the figures must be beautiful in order to pass the supreme test of being found worthy to be loved. I felt with scandalised resentment that life had somehow cheated by departing from the rules I had believed to be reliable. Our attempts to turn this first bitter disillusionment into a joke were not very successful.

The next day, Janet and I said good morning to the Eastons in a businesslike way and realised, once and for all, that it was no use expecting romance from our honeymoon couple. Out of her wedding puce and in a woollen jumper and an unbecoming short skirt, the bride looked no lovelier.

The weather was brilliantly fine, and in the sun and wind of the following week Mrs Easton's dampish pale skin quickly caught fire, so that her short-sighted eyes, when, for one interesting moment in the lounge at Sea View she removed her glasses, peered out of white circles, thrown into contrast

by the inflamed flesh along her cheekbones and the angry red dent where the nosepiece of her spectacles had rested. The behaviour of the lovers did not come up to our earlier expectations, either. At meals, they ate solidly and, so far as we could tell, hardly addressed a word to each other. In the lounge, they sat buried in detective stories, as though they had come to Mackerel Bay expressly for the purpose of having a nice read. They seemed to be a younger, more ordinary reflection of the old Rogers, seen in some mirror that had given them more hair, vulgarised their colouring, and left out the distinction age frequently hands as a consolation prize to those who have not had it bestowed on them by the world. I soon forgot the Eastons completely except for those moments before meals when I bumped into them – Mr Easton sucking a pipe and carrying his detective novel, Mrs Easton freshly and unbecomingly powdered over her high flush – coming downstairs to sit and wait silently for Mrs Marlbury's Effie to pound the gong.

One afternoon, I went with my youngest cousin, John, for a walk along the seashore – the others had gone by bus to the market town to visit the cinema – with the vague purpose of looking for shells for his collection in a certain pebbly spot, which we had always considered particularly fruitful. At this point of the beach, the sand dunes ended, and the shore became rocky and was strewn with huge, flat, wonderfully clean-looking stones and seamed with miniature canyons, into which the sea washed warmish water, shells, and swatches of glistening seaweed. On our way from Sea View, we passed

Mr and Mrs Rogers, who were sitting on a bench, he with his knees wide apart and his lips pursed as though he were whistling, she mildly nodding agreement to the crashing waves. They caught sight of us and loosed their hands, which were joined, to wave to us. John was carrying a tin bucket, and the wind seized Mr Rogers' shouted salutation and delivered it in a sort of gusty, facetious shorthand: 'Gah – an – shar – i – there?' John managed a sickly grin and a jerk of the head in reply.

When we reached the spot we were aiming for, we parted company. John skipped more quickly from stone to stone than I did, and I was not really interested in looking for shells, anyway. I preferred to dawdle at my own pace, peering into the pools, staring dreamily at the sea, and carrying on a peaceful interior conversation with myself. It was a wonderful day. The sun was almost hot when you could get out of the wind, and the sea beyond the white-capped breakers was a dark, solid-looking blue, all of a piece, without green or purple shadows. John was out of sight when I came upon the Eastons. They had taken shelter behind two large rocks that formed a convenient windbreak, and they did not see me as I came scrambling silently, in my rubber-soled shoes, across the stones and paused quite near them. Mr Easton was lying with his head in Mrs Easton's lap, and appeared to be asleep. Mrs Easton's head was tied up in a loudly patterned scarf, and her body was huddled in a lumpish, patient attitude as she looked down at her husband, who was not, after all, sleeping, for as I hesitated, peeping between the rocks, he moved his head and said something. I could not see the expression on his face as he looked up at her, but I could see hers clearly, and even to a stupid adolescent it was a revelation. Her face shone and was dazzling and perfectly unrecognisable with love – love that had about as much resemblance to the emotion I had dwelt upon so delightfully of late as the huge, glistening sea beyond the white-caps had to the small, turgid puddle of salt water beside my foot. I could not move away. I stood fascinated, staring at this humdrum little couple who, by looking into each other's unattractive faces, had told me extraordinary things about themselves, and about the old Rogers and sad, doggy Mr Stemp and the dignity of all human affection. In a muddled flash, I felt the disturbing message. Mrs Easton stooped her head. They kissed, and I turned and fled.

John appeared around some rocks and shouted at me a minute or two later. We scrambled toward each other.

'Found anything much?' he asked when we were within conversational distance.

'Nothing,' I said.

But this was not the truth. For Mackerel Bay had slipped into my hand a cold, faintly pink shell, which would sing against my ear a song without words and, I guessed, without end.

INTIMATIONS OF MORTALITY

23 August 1952

❖❖❖

My nurse Kate supplied me, as a child, with vast quantities
of tender, uncritical love, for which I was never sufficiently
grateful, although I felt that it was of a different quality from the
love bestowed on me by my parents. My father's and mother's
affection was something I had to live up to. Even in the talk of
the relatives who came to see us from time to time – mostly
country people whose eyes were a bright, milky blue, the
colour of the innocent little flowers that grow in the cornfields,
and whose sturdy bodies were dressed in rather old-fashioned
hairy tweeds, which looked and smelled, I used to imagine, as
though my relatives lived in an earthy bank under the
foxgloves with the round, good, furry creatures of the Beatrix
Potter books – even in these relatives' talk, I heard vaguely,
passed back and forth over my head, a constant assessment of
the items I had inherited from the huge, muddled store-chest
of family characteristics. In this depository, each generation
had salted away some feature as distinctive, as prevailing, as
those blue eyes, or a habit, or a trick of speech or gesture. My
love of scribbling in penny exercise books, for instance, was
not (it appeared) something that belonged to me alone but an
extension of the famous and vivacious gifts of my Aunt Violet,

whose letters were passed admiringly round the family circle, and whose account of the Delhi Durbar in 1911 had actually been published by a ladies' weekly journal. Even my face was not my own. Would I ever be as pretty as my lovely Irish mother? It was doubted by these pink-cheeked, delectable aunts, prodding me kindly, as though they were encouraging a young calf to look its best at market. Or as good-humoured as my father? More doubts, more prods, to the accompaniment of bonbons fished out of deep pockets in the tweed skirts and offered to me gently in the palms of gardening-calloused hands, much as these dear women would have offered scraps of breakfast toast to their ponies.

As for Kate, who had no similar rates of exchange to value me by, I was entered in the book of her heart simply as 'Child' – *her* child for eight years that seemed endless to me, though no doubt they passed all too quickly for her up to the sad moment when we had to part. During those years – except for one dreadful moment, which I shall relate – I am certain that I was never out of her thoughts or dreams, day or night. I had the comfortable feeling that she expected nothing of me I would not be able to give, that we knew the best and worst of each other and could relax when alone together, as one relaxes when putting on, at the end of a tiring day, an old and loved garment. I had need of the sense of stability she gave me. My father was a soldier, and our life was constantly changing its background as we moved around after him. But where I went, Kate went too, bringing with her the climate of warm, unchanging affection that I accepted with as little comment or gratitude as I accepted the sunlight when it flooded through the curtains of the series of furnished houses, in one drab military spot or another, to which I referred as 'home'.

One year, in the most exciting of all our moves, we followed my father to Ireland. Kate and I picked branches of hawthorn berries on our walks, and over the jagged coral hedges we looked toward the larkspur mountains and heard the sea birds screaming and crying weirdly on the long white strand. In such moments, when the rain fell gently, sadly, out of a sky where the clouds might suddenly be pinned together with a dazzling rainbow, my partly Irish blood felt a stir of satisfaction. But Kate was oppressed with melancholy. She would sigh, and say, 'It's hard to think of them back in old London,' and, staring at the sky, now washed bright and clear as a mirror, she would dreamily survey the domes, the crowding chimney pots and the black alleyways of that sooty Celestial City.

She cheered up, however, one evening when there was a dance at our house. On that occasion, the gala item of her attire was a white blouse, beautifully starched and ironed, through which little red ribbons could be seen coquettishly threaded in the ruchings of her camisole. They were the colour of the hawthorn berries and of her bright cheeks, which contrasted so prettily with her soft brown hair, drawn up in abundant loops on the top of her head. This finery made her look fascinating but strange to me, who had been allowed to stay up and see the gaiety, and I was furiously jealous of the young fellows who, one after another, bore her off to whirl round the floor to the music of the one-legged fiddler. But again and again her eyes returned to me, her hand waved, and I was appeased with the delicious certainty that I was always in her thoughts, however happily she footed it with her partners, and that it was toward me she would turn and walk smilingly back when the music ceased, the red ribbons heaving and the now even more vivid colour flying flags in her face.

Not long after this, we were for a short time in rooms in London, and here Kate became again a new person. When back on her native heath, her very tread seemed brisker, her mild voice sharpened, and there was a happy alertness in the lift of her head as she sniffed the acrid air. This element was composed mainly, to my recollection, of soot and fog. I might now have reflected wistfully to Kate, as we took our walks abroad, that it was hard to think of the hawthorn hedges, which must still be showing their brilliant colour in the soft, clean air of my mother's country. For here late autumn was signalled by swirling damp yellowish vapours, which curled down my throat and made my eyes smart and water.

London seemed wrapped from end to end in fog. The city was as mottled and dun-coloured as the board covers of some dirty old volume that opened here and there to disclose a thrilling illustration: the brilliant window of a toyshop in an arcade, full of gaily painted hoops and lead soldiers and curly-headed china babies, simpering under the gas jets; or maybe the doorway of some huge house where the pavement was protected by a little red-and-white striped tent and Kate said, 'The King of Spain's to be here tonight, they say'; or simply a shapeless form sidling up out of the extraordinary

substance that was London and, with a snatch of wheedling words, holding out to me from under its shawl a dirty white claw that grasped a tiny limp bunch of Parma violets. Poverty and riches were new ideas, illustrated at every turn of the great, bewildering city's streets through which Kate proudly steered me. She gazed placidly on the coughing sellers of violets, on the troops of ragged children who screamed across our tracks as piercingly as any sea birds had screamed on the empty Irish shore, on the ghosts who stood at ghostly curbs, outside stonily (as I felt) closed and warmly lighted houses, quavering ballads in voices that appeared to be the very essence of fog, but these things struck me with wonder and alarm. Her London, I discovered, was not all beautiful. Dickens was still close in those days, it seems to me now, and so were Sherlock Holmes and Moriarty. I knew none of them then, but I was glad of the warm feel of Kate's hand when we stepped out into the labyrinth of streets where I had learned, alas, that even a Celestial City has its sad citizens.

One day my parents went away to stay with friends in the country for a couple of nights. The morning after their departure, Kate received a letter – an unusual event, which I noticed particularly because of its effect on her. She read the letter several times, folding it up, unfolding it, and reading it again with a worried expression. That afternoon, she told me to button myself into the sailor reefer and put on the gold-lettered cap in which, as much as a solid female child of seven can do, I strove to give the impression of being a member of the crew of H.M.S. *Illustrious*.

‘Where are we going?’ I asked.

‘To see someone who’s ill.’

‘Oh, who?’

‘Now, don’t bother me with questions,’ said Kate sharply.

My curiosity was purely a matter of form. I had plenty to occupy my thoughts without wondering why we were about to take this expedition. Kate was unusually silent as we left the house. The fog had lifted, and it was a fine day – that is to say, a wan shaft of light struck between the houses, which were still faintly hazy, as though the monstrous bonfire of autumnal London was burning its weeds just around the corner – and the baker whistled as he pushed his little handcart up the street. Usually we went walking in the parks, but that day we stopped at the corner and boarded a bus. We rattled away through the crowded streets, past the shops, the black old churches sitting squarely among their black tombstones like hens over a clutch of sooty chicks, and the rows and rows of ugly little houses. I gazed at their windows, veiled with grubby lace curtains, in spellbound disbelief that there could ever be enough people in one town to live in them. London went on forever, it seemed. I had a perpetual fear of getting lost, and the alarming thought occurred to me that Kate might not be able to find our way back again. A glance at her matter-of-fact expression as she sat by my side – so oddly taken up with her own thoughts that for once she did not even notice I was chewing the elastic of my sailor cap – reassured me.

At last we got out of the bus, and walked for a way through a shabby district, where children were playing hopscotch on squares chalked on the pavement while women, their heads

bristling with curling pins, leaned out of their windows to chat with neighbours. The children stopped their game to stare after me, and I felt that H.M.S. *Illustrious* was coming in for a little disrespectful attention. Kate marched me into a tall, ugly brick building, and we began to climb some dirty stairs, where, through open doors on the landings, I received interesting information about the people who lived there – a broken pram, bins of garbage, and sounds of quarrelling voices. When I hung back, peeping through the doors, Kate hurried me on.

Halfway up, we stopped at a closed door, which, at Kate's knock, was opened by an old woman, and we walked into the smells – overpowering to my middle-class nostrils – of a couple of poor little rooms where a number of people were living and one was dying. There was the old woman who had let us in; her face, collapsed into the shapelessness of an old shoe by her lack of teeth, was further distorted by her rush of tearful words when she saw Kate. There were a couple of lurking children, and a thin dog with suspicious yellow eyes, lying in a box with some lumps of puppies, sleek and grey-black like tiny wet seals. On a big bed – I had difficulty in recognising this article of furniture, for it looked as bleak as a mountaintop, and the few dishevelled coverings made it seem neither cosy nor inviting – lay a woman. Or was she a woman? At first I could hardly tell that either. Kate had immediately hurried across the room to her, and I followed slowly, staring with all my eyes. I was scared but fascinated by the shiny yellow skin stretched tightly over the sharp bones, by the matted hair sticking to the brow, and by the rough breath whistling from the poor blue lips, which reminded me of the travesty of healthy colouring I sometimes gave with my water-colour paints to the ladies in the Army & Navy Stores catalogue when I supplied those dignified matrons with blue flesh and rose-blushing hair. The odours of death and poverty – a part of the sinister air of London – seeped into my lungs for the first time. I stood leaning forward slightly, so that my lips touched the cold rusty metal of one of the knobs on the foot of the bed, and waited for Kate to remember that I was there. But my Kate had disappeared. The stranger who sat in her place, holding the hand of the sick woman, seemed to be unaware of me. What was more, she was talking so rapidly and had slipped into such an easy, rough accent (as a French-woman who has been talking French with great precision out of kindness to your dull ear suddenly, and with relief, starts rattling away incomprehensibly to a compatriot who has entered the room) that I could not follow much of what she was saying. She took money out of her purse and folded the coins inside the dreadful hand, which looked like the hand of London – that claw holding out the tiny faded nosegay of Parma violets through the fog. The woman murmured something, and her head rolled over on the pillow so that her eyes stared into mine, and deep in the sockets I saw a flicker of something resembling a smile, like the dim light of a candle suddenly appearing far away down the corridor of a house one had thought was empty. I was too awed to smile back.

The old woman made some tea for us, and the children, who had gone away, returned with another person – a man, dressed in greasy overalls, as though he had slipped round

the corner from work. He and Kate talked for a while, and I watched them with a feeling of uneasiness caused by something in her face – that kind face I reckoned on finding always untroubled and ready to beam on me like the sun. As I struggled with this sensation, she stooped and kissed the sweaty yellow forehead, which stuck up like a rock on that bare plateau of bed. Before I knew where I was, Kate had bustled me to the door, and we were clattering down the stairs again and out into the fresh, the incredibly fresh, air.

Kate walked away very fast and I jogged beside her, glancing up at her face as I began to prepare a torrent of questions. None got asked, for I found that she was crying bitterly. The tears squeezed out of her eyes and ran unchecked down her cheeks. A perfect earthquake of emotions shook my heart. I was shocked to the quick to see that Kate, the source of all comfort, could shed tears, and the brave flag of my belief that grownups, by being grown up, must be happy was lowered forever. I was also disturbed by the feeling that Kate was not altogether mine, as I had thought, for she had gone miles away from me while we were in that room. I felt desolate. She brought out a handkerchief and blew her nose vigorously now; we were practically back at the main road, where we would board our homeward bus.

By the time we reached home, my overcharged heart had decided to seek relief and call attention to its own woe. I tripped over an uneven paving stone, fell, and lightly skinned my knee, which I exhibited with loud complaints. And now – out of jealousy of the strangers who had proved that Kate could forget me, and perhaps out of the sense of loss to come from an unbelievable future when she would no longer be there at all – I began to behave badly, because I so longed to show her that I loved her. I dragged my feet and grumbled and complained of feeling tired and, that night, of being hot and aching in the head. Sure enough, this autosuggestion took effect, and by the time my parents returned, the following morning, I was shivering and burning in bed with an alarmingly high temperature.

'How ever did she start this, Kate?' asked my mother. 'She was right as anything when we left.'

Kate and I looked at each other. I said nothing. 'There's a lot of this influenza about,' Kate said. We never referred to the visit we had paid together, but I often thought of it.

A year later, the unbelievable happened and Kate left us, and in time I forgot to miss her. But I know now that she was the only person in my life who loved me without wanting any return, and I hope with all my heart, though without much conviction, that the tears I saw her shed so mysteriously on that far-off day were the last she ever wept.

hypocrisy of snobs

THEIR WALK OF LIFE

12 September 1953

On their way to see the Tuppers, Horace Lessing broke a gloomy silence by saying to his wife, 'The thing that I really can*not* get over is the deception.'

'I know, dear.'

'I would never have believed it of Rosalie. As I've said before, that really is what sticks in my throat.'

Christine Lessing sighed, leaning back in the car and looking out absently at the familiar hedges and marshy fields going by. He had said it before, and so had she – countless times and in varying forms. There was really nothing left to say any longer, which was why they had left their trim white house a few minutes earlier, had got into their Austin, and were now heading toward the far less trim cottage of the Tuppers. Horace had said that if anyone passed by and noticed their car parked outside the Tuppers' hedge, it would cause no comment. He or she might easily have dropped in on some bit of village business, such as the Flower Show or the Pig Club, for, between them, they ran quite a lot of that sort of thing in the neighbourhood.

They were a middle-aged couple, busy and successful. Horace Lessing practised as a solicitor in the English seaside

town that spread its ugly suburbs inland, twenty miles away, but they preferred to live out in the country. The Lessings were accepted as part of the little community. Horace was a tall, thin man of fifty-two, with a bald forehead that was a bright pinkish brown even in winter, and with something quietly humorous in his manner that caused strangers who set him down first as a stodgy, conventional fellow to glance at him sharply and feel not quite so sure. Christine Lessing, a couple of years younger, had not achieved the dignified solution to maturity that is often to be seen in the faces of women of the Latin races. Her English prettiness had simply stayed, without anything happening beneath it, though the forget-me-nots and roses of its exterior had toned down to pot-pourri. She was a chain smoker, as the fingers of her right hand testified. She and Horace had resisted an impulse to dress up slightly for the coming interview, and had gone out 'just as they were', which meant that Horace wore an elderly dark-blue blazer and flannel trousers and that Christine's thin, active form was encased in a cotton dress of a type neither more nor less youthful than she would have worn thirty years before. Her still-reddish hair was tidy under a hair net; at the last moment she had decided against a hat.

It was getting on for evening of a lovely day in late summer. The sun, beginning to dip westward, slanted across the splendid bronze of the wheat fields, and odours of wet mint and honeysuckle, mingled with the strange, disturbing smell of the ferns, wafted out of the hedges into the Lessings' faces as they drove along. They were too preoccupied to feel pleasure in this, or even to notice it. The past few weeks had been equally beautiful, but they had been ruined for this couple ever since the day, about a month back, when their only child, Rosalie, had told them that she intended to marry a young man called George Tupper.

'But good heavens!' Christine had cried, half-laughing, half-vexed. 'George Tupper? Who *is* George Tupper?'

It had been obvious from her expression that she was running mentally over the tennis parties, the Cricket Club dances, and the other social occasions through which Rosalie had so successfully carried her bright head and well-shaped figure in the eighteen months she had been home from school.

'You know him,' Rosalie had said cheerfully. 'The Tuppers who live at that old cottage beyond the pond.'

Their hopes had crashed round their ears almost audibly, so resounding was the shock. Naturally, they had expected Rosalie to marry. She was an extremely pretty girl of eighteen, who took after Christine, but in Rosalie everything in the picture was bright and new. Her eyes glistened, and so did her short, square white teeth, and so did her lips, and her mane of light-red hair. Everything about her glistened delightfully, like a leaf on a fresh summer morning. Horace had some-times thought, with a touch of melancholy, that it would not be long before she was married to one of the nice youngsters who ran her around to parties and tennis. It had not occurred to him to look for his future son-in-law in a ditch, which was where he remembered last seeing George Tupper, one day not long ago as he was driving along the road toward his office. The young man had been standing knee-deep in bracken, slashing away with a billhook at a rough bank; he worked for the rural district council on the roads. Horace had glanced at him as he drove by, indifferently registering his presence, as though young Tupper were a stone or a haystack by the roadside. It gave him a strange feeling now to think how that stone, that haystack, was looming so large in his life.

The parents, keeping themselves well in hand, had asked Rosalie how she happened to meet George Tupper in the first place, for as far as they knew, the young couple had not exchanged a word. Then it had come out – the first casual encounter, the long deception. Rosalie's bicycle tyre had been punctured, and, emerging from the cow parsley like antique Love rising from the warm Cyprian sea, George Tupper had mended it for her. They had met again along the road soon afterward, and Rosalie got off her bicycle and stopped for a chat. There had been an instant attraction between them; for nearly a year since that time they had been meeting regularly. When Rosalie took her tennis racket and went off, as the Lessings understood, to play singles with her best friend, the doctor's daughter, she had really been going to meet George in some wood. When she whistled to Christine's two cairn terriers and strode off down the lane in her tweed skirt and jersey, the little dogs yapping with excitement round her rather large but seductive legs, she had been less intent on exercise than on meeting a lover. It was bad luck, Horace had grimly reflected, that the fellow was not confined between four walls for at least part of the day, but he worked under the sky, along the highroad, among the common nettles, always and infernally accessible.

The Lessings were shaken to think that with their daughter living at home, at such close quarters, they had not had the slightest suspicion anything was going on. They were badly hurt by her extraordinary deceit, for they had believed in their innocent hearts that she told them everything. That day, when she did at last tell them, they had asked her if anyone else had heard about it.

Rosalie showed her lovely strong teeth in a delightful laugh. 'I don't think we've even been seen together,' she said. She looked as candid as the dawn sky.

'Thank goodness,' Christine said.

'Everyone will know soon, of course. George is going to tell his mother and father today, too.'

'Well, ask them to keep the – the information to themselves for the time being,' said Horace sharply.

He had boggled at the word 'news', which would seem to give an official ring of confirmation.

'But not for long,' Rosalie protested. 'We want to get married as soon as we can.'

'Does he make enough to keep you on?' her father had then asked.

'Well, he's thinking of changing his job. We'd get a house with the new one.'

'There's a lot to talk over first,' Christine said.

Rosalie had looked smilingly from one to the other. 'Talk away!' she said amiably.

It struck Horace, in the days which followed, that for the rest of his life he would feel a nagging worry whenever he smelled the sweet smell of cooking fruit and sugar. It was the time of year when Christine and their cook, Harriet, made household preserves, and every evening when he entered the house and hung up his hat in the hall, he met the warm smell of hot plum jam or damson cheese or crab-apple jelly. In the restless energy of her unhappiness, Christine was making jams as other women, also wretched, might buy new clothes, or take a lover, or go off on a long, uncomfortable journey. Horace wondered how they would ever eat their way through the shelves and shelves of his wife's misery. Rosalie kept herself tactfully out of the way much of the time. She went about with her friends, played tennis, joined parties to go swimming in the river from a friend's boat-house, and they heard her singing and whistling merrily when she was at home.

Horace and Christine had talked without ceasing, in these fine late-summer days, which passed in anxiety and the fragrance of jam floating from the kitchen. Christine would come out into the hall, fishing in the pocket of her purple-splashed apron for her packet of cigarettes, and almost immediately they would start their discussion. They were at their wit's end. In their circle, people did not marry out of 'their walk of life', as Christine called it. When she said the phrase, it was possible to imagine that she was thinking about a neat, tree-lined avenue, bordered with comfortable-looking houses approximately the size of the Lessings' and leading on, without a swerve or a kink, toward a placid horizon. The world had changed, as Horace was ready to acknowledge, but it had not changed that much. The Lessings were humiliated when they imagined the comments of their friends whose

daughters had not chosen to look over the hedge and fall in love with a labourer. They struggled to face their predicament in a sensible, modern way, but the painful fact remained that Rosalie wished to marry a man whose father could neither read nor write, who probably read nothing himself but the football pools and whose resources in all ways seemed so limited that Horace, made cynically aware of the frailty of human nature by his professional experience, could only shake his head and prophesy disaster. When he and Christine thought of Rosalie stuck in some dreadful cottage, working from dawn to dusk and breeding like a rabbit, no doubt, they were filled with horror.

Horace had suggested to Rosalie that George Tupper might come along for a glass of sherry one evening. He told her that Thursday would be suitable, hoping she would not instantly detect that it was suitable because Harriet on that day always crammed herself into her good blue costume, took her umbrella with the bulldog's-head handle, and half a dozen eggs in a cardboard shoe box, and went on the bus into town to see her married niece. Horace did not like the idea that he was being forced to be deceitful, too, but he wanted to be sure that there would be no gossip.

George had come. He had put on a neat brown suit and slicked back his hair with water. His Adam's apple looked as though it were uneasy at being made captive by a collar and tie. Horace and Christine had studied him with intense curiosity, for they both felt that his face as they remembered it must be an imperfect recollection, and that the reality would supply them with clues to their private disaster. To their amazement, as they agreed afterward, it appeared exactly the same. He was really an ordinary-looking young man, with a bumpy forehead, and sandy eyelashes tipped with lighter gold. Red had called to red; Rosalie's beautiful, clear, Venetian colouring had attracted George's honest ginger. Horace, while he rattled nervously about at the tray of decanters and glasses, had found himself wondering absently about their children, who would be red as little foxes.

'Drink up – you're being very slow,' he'd said, and young Tupper had started, and then thrown the sherry down his throat with violence.

The Lessings had hoped that the sight of George perhaps appearing to less advantage in the surroundings of her own home might give Rosalie pause. After an early attack of fidgeting, the young man had appeared collected. He sat munching a genteel cocktail biscuit. His hands were small but strong, and his nails were dirty. The parents looked at Rosalie. She was gazing at her lover with a contented smile. Their quietness together, which seemed to be full of certainty, began to alarm Horace. He asked George about his new job. The young man was going to work for a farmer two villages away.

'That's a *very* sensible idea,' Christine said, with a thin smile.

'I hitched up with him on account of him offering a cottage,' George said. 'The last man left it pretty mucky – his wife was in hospital half the time – but it's modern. Main light and a cesspool.'

'A *lovely* cesspool,' Rosalie said.

George laughed. 'It won't be too bad for a start, Rozzie thinks. I'm going over evenings to start putting it right.'

Christine looked at Horace. He cleared his throat and made a dry little speech, to which the young couple listened without interrupting.

Then George had said calmly, 'Well, if you think we must wait, Mr Lessing, I reckon there isn't anything to be done about it.'

'I'm sorry, but we shall never give our consent,' Christine said, on a firm note.

'But we'll lose the cottage,' Rosalie wailed. 'It's for a married man. George said he was going to be married soon.'

'Can't be helped, Rozzie,' George said.

He seemed entirely unruffled. Rosalie went with him to the gate, and stood talking busily while he put on his bicycle clips. Then he wheeled out his bike and rode away. With a disturbing serenity, Rosalie came back to the house, humming a gay little tune.

It was a few days later, while Rosalie was away for a brief visit with a school friend, that her parents had decided to go and have a straight talk with the Tuppers. George had already left for his new job. Now, as they drove along between the fragrant hedgerows, which fanned soft puffs of intoxicating sweetness into their unheeding faces, Horace tried to comfort himself with the thought that Tupper, illiterate old man though he was, might have the horse sense to realise better than his son that there was nothing doing. If George and Rosalie waited until Rosalie was twenty-one and legally of age, then Horace would have to wash his hands of them both. But he proposed to offer to help George emigrate – alone, of course. Otherwise, the situation would be perfectly intolerable. They would have to move from the neighbourhood where they were so well liked and respected, for the Tuppers couldn't be trusted to keep their mouths shut. Old Tupper would get excited one night and start to brag in the Barley Sheaf. At the thought, Horace gave a loud, exasperated grunt and sharply struck the palm of his left hand on the steering wheel.

'What?' said Christine, startled.

'Oh, nothing. Here we are.'

He parked the car close to the ragged hedge, and they got out and walked up the path to the Tuppers' cottage. One or two hens stopped giving back-kicks in the earth under the currant bushes and gazed at the visitors inquisitively. There was no one about; the rest of the Tuppers' sons and daughters were married and gone. Horace lifted his hand and rapped sharply on the door. In a minute, there were heavy steps, and Mrs Tupper opened it. 'Come in, Mrs Lessing. Come in, sir.'

She was a fat woman with a waterfall of chins tumbling to a high, full bosom, which, in its exposed upper reaches, looked polished, hard, and brown as walnut. Christine walked quickly past her, followed by Horace.

'In here,' Mrs Tupper said. 'Father's in the kitchen.'

She opened a door and showed them into the little front best room, which struck cold to the flesh after the warm evening air outside.

'We'd like a chat with you and Mr Tupper,' Christine said nervously.

'He's just finished his tea. I'll get him,' said Mrs Tupper. She left the room.

The Lessings sat down, side by side, on a horsehair sofa. In spite of the fireplace, in which a fan of orange paper was crinkled realistically, the smell of the room was damp. They said nothing until Mrs Tupper returned with her husband. Tupper was still in his working clothes, and resembled a stiff, creaking parcel tied up at various points with string. He was wiping his mouth with the back of his hand.

'Evening, Mr Lessing,' he said.

He and his wife sat down on two chairs facing the Lessings. The room was so narrow that the four of them, sitting upright, resembled four strangers mistrustfully eyeing each other across a railway carriage that had got shunted, by some accident of travel, into a siding. Horace's flannel-covered knee was practically touching Tupper's corduroy one.

'I daresay you can guess why we want to see you,' Horace said.

'About our George,' Tupper said. He looked slyly from Horace to Christine. He had a big, streaky grey moustache, with ginger ends that looked stained, as though they had been dipped in strong tea. His forehead was bumpy like George's, Christine noticed with a feeling of distaste.

Horace began to speak. The Tuppers listened silently. Mrs Tupper had adopted what was evidently a habitual attitude, one arm, across her bosom, supporting the elbow of her other arm, and the fingers of the supported hand splayed to the side of her cheek, as though she were clapping a poultice to some aching spot there.

'Can't say as how we're keen on it neither, Mr Lessing,' Tupper said, at last, when Horace paused for breath and looked expectantly at him.

'You're not keen?' Christine said sharply.

Mrs Tupper shook her head sadly, still propping her soft cheek and chins under the invisible poultice. 'Oh, it isn't right, is it, Father?' she said, looking at her husband.

'No, it isn't,' Tupper said.

'George ought to have known better. That's what Father and me thinks.'

Horace stammered slightly when he was moved or angry. Now, with that hesitation in his speech, he said ironically, 'I should have thought he was doing pr-pretty well.'

'A wife makes a difference to a boy like George,' Tupper said. 'Just making his way, like, and your girl – well, it don't do, Mr Lessing.'

Quelling an indignant movement from Christine with a warning glance, Horace asked, 'Then I take it you haven't told anyone yet?'

'Haven't said nothing to nobody,' Tupper said. 'We don't want no talk.'

'I am very glad indeed that you're being so sensible,' Horace said. He felt perfectly furious.

The Lessings talked for a little while longer before getting up to go. Horace had finally made his offer to help George emigrate.

'So you'll tell your son what I've said' were his parting words. 'You'll do your best to make him see reason?'

'Yes,' Tupper said. He shot out a hand and took hold of

Horace's blazer. He was the shorter man of the two, and he looked up into Horace's face with a strange, gentle smile. 'But it won't do no good. They'll marry.' He gave the pleat of dark-blue blazer a little shake. 'They'll marry, sure enough, and there aren't a thing to be said that'll stop 'em.'

Horace and Christine climbed into the Austin and drove home. On the way, they said hardly anything. When they reached the house, Christine said that she had a headache and would go upstairs and take some aspirin. Horace, after he had put the car in the garage, wandered rather aimlessly into the garden. Everything looked very neat. The lawns were freshly mown, and the second crop of roses was coming into flower. Horace loved his roses, but he looked at them abstractedly. He was thinking of Tupper's eyes and his smile as he said, 'They'll marry, sure enough.' And suddenly Horace knew that Tupper was right and that there was nothing to be done. He gave up. He had beaten his head against the hard fact in vain, refusing to believe it, until a stupid old man had taken hold of him by the coat, and, lo! it was so.

Horace looked up at the evening sky, which looked steadily back, appearing to say 'Well?' And really he did not know. In the confusion of his thoughts, all he knew for certain was that his grandchildren would be red as little foxes, playing round his feet. Poor Christine and her walk of life! Rosalie had jumped out of it, all right, and was it so important? He felt muddled about everything. He had a peculiar feeling when he thought of Rosalie and George. Was it envy? He did not know that, either. He started to walk round his well-kept garden, pausing to snip off a flower head or to rub a scented leaf between his fingers, postponing the moment when he would go in and tell Christine that she must dry her eyes and start thinking about the wedding.

pointlessness of doing everything 'right': how exhausting!

THE WILLOUGHBYS

2 October 1954

Chance friendships that begin on a holiday very seldom survive in the less genial and expansive air of everyday life. They have something in common with the delicate rosy shells, the strange pebbles, and the swatches of glistening, rubbery, frilled seaweed that, as children on the beach, we collect with such care and carry home, where, mysteriously, they lose their colours with their shine, and are quickly thrown away.

The Willoughbys were an exception to the rule. I met the three of them – mother, son, and daughter – in a small mountain hotel in Austria, where I was passing a few summer weeks, and I continued to see something of them after we all returned to London. The trio first became of interest to me in the hotel dining room, a long, narrow apartment, partly glassed in like a conservatory, against which some big trees in the garden pressed so closely that they seemed to be stooping their green heads to see what we were getting to eat. The light in this room was filtered through their boughs, and the effect was always of a cool, translucent aquarium, in which the faces of the guests swam like fish. I sat, a single woman at a little table near the wall, with nothing to do but watch the other inhabitants at their meals.

I would have remembered the Willoughbys' faces perfectly if I had never seen them again. There is something perverse about memory, which rejects so many important things yet picks up, as the hem of a coat will pick up a burr, the impression of some stranger watched for weeks or days, or even a few hours, in a hotel or on a ship. Perhaps it is when one is slightly bored that the burrs begin sticking to the fibres of the memory. Probably I saw the Willoughbys with that intense, slightly abnormal holiday vision, but they were rather striking in themselves. I watched them across the room for some days before any of us exchanged a word, and by the end of that time they had caught, they had clung. Try as I would, I should not be able quite to brush these total strangers away.

In the first place, Mrs Willoughby and her grown-up children all looked extremely English. When they arrived, in their good tweeds, there were few English visitors staying in the hotel. Among the other guests who stamped in hungrily in their nailed boots each mealtime, the Willoughbys were unmistakable. Mrs Willoughby and her son were almost comically alike. She was a woman of about fifty-five. He was in his early thirties, I judged. They were both slim, handsome, elegant, and nervous. Their noses were also peculiarly English, being very straight, pinched bridges of bone across which the fine skin was tightly stretched, with a suggestion of alertness that made one feel they used these features as an insect uses its antennae. Eating is sometimes rather revealing, and both mother and son ate in nervous, quick mouthfuls, picking suspiciously at the food and often leaving their plates practically untouched. Then he would lean back and offer her

a cigarette, which she would take and fit into a long ivory holder with precise movements of her well-shaped, blue-veined hands. It was evident that perfect accord existed between the pair. Sometimes he seemed to be teasing her fondly. Occasionally, glancing coolly round the tables in the dining room, he would murmur something that was evidently amusing at the expense of some of the other visitors. At such times, when their eyes sparkled and their noses appeared to sharpen, their resemblance to one another was ridiculous.

Speculations about the Willoughbys accompanied me on my walks and amused my solitary meals. At first, I thought that the young woman at their table could not be Mrs Willoughby's daughter, but one day I heard her exclaim 'Oh, Mummy, you've dropped your scarf!' as they rose to go after luncheon. Miss Willoughby was fat and jolly. Her nose was undistinguished, her cheeks were round and pink, and her flesh was pushed out in a soft bulge over her girdle. There was no suggestion of a delicate appetite in Miss Willoughby's performance at meals. She sat between those twin grey-hounds and tucked into everything in sight. She watched the waitress coming down the dining room with the dishes for their table, and if she recognised something she liked, her blue eyes shone.

The brother and sister seemed to get on very well, too. When he pricked up his nose and made one of those (I feared) devastatingly critical remarks about their fellow-guests, she would look at him adoringly. They would stroll down the tiny village to post their postcards, her hand in his arm. It was pleasant to see them.

The weather had been dull, but suddenly, after the Willoughbys arrived, it turned hot and beautiful. The sky was the colour of gentians, and a deep, happy grasshopper chorus scraped away without ceasing in the meadow grass. The Willoughbys shed their tweeds. The mother and daughter appeared in charming linen dresses, and the son, like all the other men in the hotel, wore shorts and an open-necked shirt – but shorts and shirt with an elegant difference. The whole family was always perfectly turned out, though Miss Willoughby was apt to look slightly crumpled as the day went on.

She and I spoke to each other first. It was my ambition to speak to no one, to rest and read, and to spend hours stretched out in the sun on the sweet-smelling turf, high up in some rock-sheltered spot on the mountain slopes. But one evening I met Miss Willoughby, also going down the track back to the hotel after a solitary walk, and we fell into step together. That night as I was going through the little room, lined with clean brown wood like a cigar box, where the guests sat after dinner, the Willoughbys stopped me and asked me to join them for coffee and a brandy. So far as I knew, they had not spoken to another soul in the hotel. Either Miss Willoughby had reported favourably or they had decided that the correct English interval that must be observed before overtures are made to a stranger was now over.

'Oh, do join us! We're longing to talk,' the daughter said, patting the seat beside her and smiling.

I sat down.

When I looked at Mrs Willoughby face to face, and did not study merely her distinguished profile view in the green,

underwater light of the dining room, I thought that her expression was somewhat petulant. It was not reconciled to something or other. Somewhere, life had disappointed. Though she was gracious, her glance raked one from head to foot in a cold, expert flash of appraisal. Behind those dark eyes, with their arched lids, a little sum of evaluation had taken place. Edward, the son, had exactly the same trick of looking one swiftly up and down, charming but wary, not yet sure if it was all right. Betty Willoughby welcomed me without reserve, friendly as a puppy. I supposed that she took after the absent or dead Mr Willoughby, for she seemed to have no point of resemblance to either her mother or her brother.

We talked of London, of people, of concerts (Mrs Willoughby and Edward were, it appeared, devoted to music), of books. They pointed their noses inquiringly toward me, and I felt that they were getting their bearings on me with the help of these preternaturally gifted features. We discovered friends in common, and Mrs Willoughby became markedly more cordial. It was so easy to go wrong. Their own opinions were all beautifully 'right', like their clothes and their address. They were quick to explain why they were here, in this idyllic but far from fashionable spot. They had heard from friends that the hotel was good and reasonable, and, of course, it was 'right' not to have too much spare money or to wish to go to a more luxurious hostelry. The people one met in such places were terrible, Mrs Willoughby said. She told an amusing story about staying with a rich friend in Venice the summer before. She and Edward both had a sharp malice that made me wonder, while I laughed, exactly how they would set about carving me up after I left them.

'We're going to be energetic and try the glacier tomorrow,' Betty said. 'Why don't you come along? It would be fun.'

'I promise to carry your sandwiches,' Edward said. The evening had been quite a success. There was a modest sense of congratulation in the air.

I refused the glacier invitation, having my own reasons for being wary with kind people in hotels. It is difficult, however, to avoid catching someone's eye across a narrow glass tank of a dining room or across a cigar box of a sitting room. Next evening, the Willoughbys wanted to talk about their climb. Betty's face and neck were flaming with sunburn, but the sallow skins of her mother and brother had only acquired a warmer tan. Mrs Willoughby looked extremely handsome, the extra glow in her cheeks setting off the silver blue of her carefully waved hair. Edward had broken off two or three coral-coloured geranium heads from a hanging basket on the hotel veranda; she took them from him and tucked them into the neck of the white dress she was wearing, and they became her very well.

I liked her and Edward better that evening. They were less suspicious and therefore more relaxed, and their talk was entertaining. They played up to each other all the time. Betty kept looking from Edward to her mother, and then at me, with a fond, beaming expression of pride, as though to say, 'There! Aren't they really wonderful?'

I saw a good deal of the Willoughbys in the remaining two weeks of my stay. They were far too sensitive to be intrusive, but they threw out little invitations now and then, and I found myself accepting them. We took picnics and walks together, and twice we explored the valleys in their car. The days smelled of hay, apples, and geranium leaves, the nights of snow off the glacier glittering at the head of our valley in the light of a moon that was like an apricot. When I left – the Willoughbys had a few days longer to stay – we parted with firm promises to meet again in London.

Mrs Willoughby invited me to dinner not long after they got back. I had, of course, filled in all the missing details about them by now. Mr Willoughby was dead, and Edward and Betty made their home with their mother. Edward was a barrister; with that nose, I thought, it was easy to imagine him worming the truth out of a witness. Betty was thirty-one – two years younger than her brother – and had a secretarial job of some sort. I felt curious to see them all in their own surroundings. It is always an adjustment, meeting people after a holiday on which one has made their acquaintance for the first time. With their bare legs and arms shrouded in dark city clothes, their sunburn beginning to fade, and everyday preoccupations visibly taking charge of their thoughts once more, they are apt to seem like strangers whom one must get to know all over again.

The Willoughbys had merely changed one set of becoming clothes for another, in which they settled against their native background as gracefully as they had against the mountains and the rushing torrents of green glacier water. Their house was a Regency cottage at the entrance of a mews, in St. John's Wood. The exterior was prettily dolled up with paint and sun blinds. Inside, it was perfection, though in the faintly lifeless manner of an illustration in an interior decorating magazine. You could not imagine putting your feet up on the little striped sofa, or leaving a wet umbrella or untidy bundles in the hall, but the Willoughbys had been very artful in choosing their pieces of furniture, all of which were absolutely 'right', well bred, and charmingly arranged. The taste was excellent, and there was so much of it that it seemed actually present in the air, like a curious, depressing gas that would make you yawn after a while.

The dinner was admirable, too. I suppose most of their money went on the good address and their pretty things, for Mrs Willoughby, I discovered, had cooked the meal. I could understand why she and Edward had been so finicky with the food in Austria; her own was incomparably better. There were two other guests, as carefully chosen as the furniture. Conversation went along very pleasantly. It struck me that Edward, directly he got back to London, must have run out and bought all the well-reviewed new books and tickets for the latest plays, as a naked man would send out hastily for clothes to cover his nudity, for he was wonderfully well equipped with a wardrobe of neat opinions on everything that was going. He and Mrs Willoughby were in fine mettlesome form. The simple mountain hotel and the pastoral scene had not been right for them. London was their field of reference, and their home fitted them, exactly as a nest woven of twigs and hair would fit a couple of darting birds.

Betty and I talked for a bit after dinner. She was the only one of our holiday party who offered visible proof of having been in Arcady. Her freckled skin was still pink and peeling, and I had noticed with pleasure at dinner that she had not lost her hearty mountain appetite. Even her fatness seemed puppy fat, a soft, babyish padding that, one caught oneself thinking optimistically, must fine down before very long. The Austrian sunshine had bleached her brown hair, which was soft and babyish, too.

'Isn't it awful to be back?' she said. 'I just loved it there.'

'Don't you like London?' I asked.

'Well, I do, of course. But there was always something to do in Austria, wasn't there? What I call *do*, I mean. My job's fearfully boring.'

She sighed, sitting clumsily hunched on a black-and-gold Empire stool, with her arms embracing her knees, so that her chiffon dress was crushed. For a moment, her cheerful face looked quite woebegone, and her sunburned hands, which on our mountain outings had seemed so businesslike as they gripped a hold in the rocks or used a bottle opener or smoothed out a map, were clasped limply against the folds of blue chiffon.

The Willoughbys and I kept up in a sort of way after this reunion. I saw them no longer as sharply cut, absorbing figures, highlighted by their isolation and my own idleness. They had now sunk back into proper perspective as three people whom I had met on a holiday and did not really want to see a great deal of, I discovered, now that we had met again at home. I forgot about them for long stretches of time. But they clung, all the same, like burrs. Betty lunched with me once or twice; I liked her the best of the three. When I saw Mrs Willoughby and Edward, I had to admit that they were excellent company, and when I noticed yet again how devoted they were to each other, my heart smote me. I felt guilty for not liking them more. Sometimes after a rather lengthy period when I had not seen any of them, I would run into Mrs Willoughby in the street or meet Edward at someone else's house, as though memory were jogging my elbow and offering the Willoughbys like something I had left behind in a shop.

When I heard from a friend who was also a friend of the Willoughbys that Betty Willoughby was engaged to be married, I was surprised and pleased. It is always difficult for one woman to say to what degree another woman is attractive or unattractive to men; at any rate, a series of shocks is apt to follow any such highhanded evaluation. I had about decided in my mind, however, that the Willoughby daughter would not marry – not because her fat jolliness was definitely unpleasing, but because she seemed such a happy part of that tight little family trio. They were so absorbed in one another. I was intrigued to hear that an outsider had been admitted to their closed circle, and I was still more intrigued when I met Betty's betrothed, Fred Gates, at a small party at the Willoughbys' house.

I wondered, first of all, where Betty had met him. She lived, it had often struck me, an existence of childlike dependence and docility, roped to the other two and never scrambling off on any excursions of her own. But perhaps I had been wrong, for Edward replied in a curt undertone, 'Oh, she picked him up somewhere – God knows where.' I felt that this was an exaggeration, for, of course, not only God but Edward and Mrs Willoughby knew where. They would immediately make it their business to find out. They would point their intelligent noses at poor Betty and her love, and draw information out of the very air.

But Edward's phrase did marvellously conjure up a picture of Betty coming in out of a dark night, dropping Fred down on the mushroom-coloured carpet of their little house, and stubbornly refusing to explain, to excuse, or to eject her find. It dawned on me that though I had always thought of her as easy-going and good-humoured, she must be capable of an amazing obstinacy. There are, of course, few objections that can be raised when a woman of thirty-one announces that she has made her choice and proceeds to follow it, but I could guess what heavy batteries of malice and sarcasm Betty's mother and brother had rolled up into the front line. Though they may have wounded, they had not been able to force a retreat. She had stood firm, a changed being, made bold and resolute by love. When I followed the direction of Edward's furious glare to Fred Gates, sitting on Mrs Willoughby's striped sofa, and then glanced at Betty, who was sitting beside her lover, I thought that the pride in her face as she exhibited her own exclusive possession was extremely touching.

Fred Gates was a North Country businessman in his late forties, already with a little potbelly that strained at his waistcoat buttons as he sat spilling cigarette ash messily down it. He was badly dressed, and I noticed that this seemed to have provoked a joyful answering trill, so to speak, of dowdiness from Betty, who wore, for the first time since I had known her, a really unbecoming dress. He looked as though he would enjoy the pleasures of the table. I could imagine him and Betty, napkins tucked under their stout chins, sitting on either side of a loaded board and plying their knives and forks with the gusto of a couple of rustic diners in a Rowlandson drawing. His mouth was good-tempered, and strongly marked at the corners by little, kind half-crescent lines of laughter, and his small brown eyes surveyed the Willoughbys and their friends with a sort of practised, humorous toughness. I felt that Betty had done very well.

She thought so, plainly. She glowed with happiness as she sat beside him, her left hand (with a fat and somehow remarkably hideous diamond on the third finger) resting peacefully on his knee. Whenever he said something, in his slow Lancashire voice, she turned on the rest of us the same look – shy, swimming with emotion, yet certain of our approval and admiration – that Mrs Willoughby's and Edward's smart repartee used to evoke in the sitting room of the mountain hotel. It was obviously almost more than her mother and brother could endure, but I was pretty certain that she did not notice their expressions. What was still more extraordinary was Fred's effect on the Willoughbys' careful décor. Mrs Willoughby's drawing room, in which all the things were so perfectly 'right' that they cancelled each other out and the mind swam in period vacancy, positively drew back, wincing like Edward and Mrs Willoughby. As he sat there, telling with a beautiful broad gift for mimicry a couple of extremely funny, ribald Lancashire stories, he seemed the bold risk, the lovable, vulgar bloomer, the room had so knowingly avoided. The

other guests were visibly affected by the change. They had started off by looking at Fred Gates out of the corners of their eyes and talking quickly and lightly of things he knew nothing about and people who were strangers to him. Now they began to laugh and talk loudly, slumping back on the frail furniture as though on shabby leather chairs in a gun room.

It was a fearful disaster for them, with their ingrained habit of being always on the side of the angels in taste, of avoiding everything that was not all right, and waiting to be sure before they plunged into anything, whether it was an opinion or the colour of their dining room walls. It was, moreover, disaster of a peculiarly humiliating kind that Betty should have blundered off by herself somewhere and returned, foolishly triumphant, with a Fred Gates. Their real defeat, I thought, would be that she did not know what she had so appallingly and joyously done. I caught Edward's cold look of horror repeated, and then instantly suppressed, on Mrs Willoughby's handsome face. At one moment, just before I left, she happened to be standing beside Fred, and I saw him turn, roaring with laughter, and deal her a jovial whack on the rump. She took it admirably. Her expression and Edward's were wonderful to see, though. Mother and son were absolutely at a loss, for the first time in my acquaintance with them.

Betty followed me to the door, babbling of the wedding. 'I'm going to wear white – do you think I'll look a fool? Mummy and Edward wanted us to be married quietly in a registry office, but I don't see why one shouldn't have the whole thing for once in one's life, do you?'

'Indeed I don't,' I said.

As it happened, I was again out of England when they married. I heard later that Edward had given Betty away – and how like a martyr he would have been I could well imagine – and that the bridegroom had gone round genially telling people not to be frightened of the champagne, since it wasn't 'the usual mucky stuff'. It was delicately to be assumed that he had paid for it. The wedding had been a huge success – not because of the champagne, but on account of some quality that had shone in the faces of the somewhat ludicrous pair and spread its warmth intoxicatingly to all hearts.

So that was the end of the Willoughbys for me, I thought. At last I was free of a really rather unsatisfactory association that had continued to turn up like a dusty sprig of edelweiss brought back from a holiday and placed carelessly in the pages of a book – a souvenir that one intends to throw out but that still tumbles into one's lap at odd intervals.

But it was not quite the end, for there was one last flash of Mrs Willoughby's face, suddenly before me at some crowded function, perhaps a year later, like a ghost, and reminding me of the green aquarium wash of our mountain dining room.

I asked after Edward. He was well, very busy, beginning to be very successful.

And Betty?

'Oh, she's well, and awfully happy.' Mrs Willoughby gave me a stare; her fine nose appeared to sharpen, and bewilderment passed almost like tears over her eyes. 'Wonderfully happy!'

Forlorn, she sounded. Forlorn, I thought, the very word is like a bell, but it tolled me back to nothing. With finality and without sorrow, as though we were parting – as, after all, we should have done – on the steps of the little hotel under the glacier, we said goodbye.

THE EMPTY PLACE

27 March 1965

◆◆◇◆◆

It was very ordinary, really. A small, elderly artist, leading a
pet dog, was knocked down by a car one damp, misty evening
on Chelsea Embankment, when the reflections of the street
lamps quivered confusingly in the glassy surfaces of the roads
after heavy rain, which had fallen earlier in the afternoon.
Two days later, without regaining consciousness, Cyril
Turville died in hospital. The papers are full of such things.
They happen all the time. The young man who had driven
the car was exonerated when he described – and a handy
witness confirmed – how the tiny grey shape of Mr Turville,
attached to a grey canine shadow, had walked off the kerb
right under his wheels. Everybody knew how absent-minded
Cyril had become. The kindly young man was upset, however.
He stooped over Mrs Turville after the inquest, his fresh
forehead frowning, and looked into her face as though
debating within himself what he could say to express his
regret that he and the double wraith of man and dog should
have been magnetised toward each other that spring evening.
He said a few cautious words and went out of Dolly Turville's
life, having been the means of cutting it in two.

This unexceptional event spread a shock of dismay among
the Turvilles' friends, who had not thought of them in separate

pieces. They had been one so long and so remarkably that the sudden termination of their marriage by a moving mass of vulgar metal gave everyone a sense of outrage as well as loss. By rights, they should have met the fate of devoted couples in ancient mythology who, after a quiet, united dissolution, continued in some sort of twining vegetable partnership as adjacent trees or vines. Instead, there was that sickening, solitary crunch on the Embankment – horrible! It was only a chance that Dolly had not been sharing their usual stroll; she was nursing a cold at home. Perhaps it would almost have been better, the friends considered, if this had not been so. As telephones rang from house to house, everybody experienced the sense of sad blankness that follows the ending of something good. The delightful little Turvilles, who were like nobody else in the world, had come to an end.

Their endearing effect on all who met them had always begun, of course, with their appearance, which was quaint. They were both exceptionally small people, delicately made and altogether in perfect proportion, like a couple of those minuscule, prized pieces of furniture that precisely repeat the scale of the full-sized Chippendale bureau or chair. The Turvilles gave the impression of having been matched up with infinite care. There was nothing in their looks of either the midget or the child, though people who met them for the first time sometimes wondered if Cyril's narrow, burnished boots came from the juvenile department of some store. He was actually rather a dandy, with beautifully cut clothes and a ribboned monocle, behind which he would banish his shortsighted left eye. His eyes had an expression of peculiar sweetness, a gentle goodness, which made people take to him on sight and tell him things that they would not have told anyone else. He was asked frequently for help, and always gave it. Everybody loved Cyril. They were very fond of poor little Dolly, too, but he was the strong one.

Dolly was a helpless, pretty creature, still having retained in middle age the exquisite, seemingly boneless paws of hands and the flaming hair (now improbably tinted, it was true) that had appeared in a whole numbered 'Dolly' series of Turville portraits. They had no children; instead they had cherished a sequence of a breed of silky-haired dogs, the last of which had accompanied Cyril on the final airing along the Embankment. The Turvilles' house, in a Chelsea cul-de-sac, was part of the charming joke, being diminutive and frail, like them, and furnished with admirable eighteenth-century bits that Dolly, who had a feeling for such things, had picked up cleverly for nothing much through the years. All the pieces were scaled to the small rooms and their owners. Visitors would experience a sense of entering Lilliput as they sat down and gazed out at the postage-stamp square of back yard where on summer evenings Dolly was to be found, engulfed in an old apron, scratching away among the plants with a pickle fork. The Turvilles were always to be found by their friends, and always welcoming. Cyril's studio was just round the corner. He specialised in painting beautiful women with their children and pets; all, when he had finished with them, seemed to be composed of prettily tinted, impervious plaster of Paris. Yet he was much in demand. The supply of husbands who admired these compositions appeared to be endless.

The problem of Dolly's future loomed large in many people's minds after they heard the news. First of all, there were the awful formalities to be got through. The sight of Cyril's coffin at the cremation was nearly too much for Eileen Scoby, as for many others. Its size – pathetically neat, almost bijou, one might say – brought him back so vividly. He had been a little angel of sweetness, Miss Scoby reflected – really a saint! In all the years, she had never known him ruffled or out of temper. When it slid unobtrusively out of sight, as the modest little man himself would have done, she glanced surreptitiously at Dolly. The Turvilles had been oddly bare of relations – it increased the feeling that they had sprung into being solely to exist for one another – and the widow knelt between Eileen and her brother, Mervyn Scoby, their oldest friends. The Scobys' shoulders hemmed her in like a tiny, quiet prisoner between two warders.

'She is being wonderful, really,' Eileen said to Scoby on the way home. They had just seen two other friends put Mrs Turville into their car, talking cheerfully, and drive off with her on the front seat beside the husband while the wife, afflicted by the well-meaning dementia that often seizes people on such occasions, kept up a flow of brisk babble from the rear. They were taking her home to Kent for a few days, or as long as she wished to stay.

'That's not unusual at first,' her brother answered.

Scoby was a solicitor, a dry-looking man with a scatter of liver-coloured freckles peppering the bald spot on his crown.

'I know. When there won't be things to settle and she can sit down and think – that's the worst time, everybody says.'

'She'll have to start thinking at once, I'm afraid,' he said as they went up the steps of the house in a Chelsea square they had long and amicably shared. 'Things won't be all that easy.'

Once inside, he went straight to the cupboard where he kept the drinks, and mixed two large whiskies, though they usually took little before lunch. They needed something this morning. Scoby, the glass in his hand, stood staring out at the gardens of the square, where a blackbird was singing lustily in the sunshine. Eileen had departed with her drink to put their cold lunch on the table. He took a swallow of the whisky and thought of poor Dolly being whirled out of London on a wave of determined good cheer. He had been deeply in love with her many years before, and his friends had taken it for granted that it was because of this unrewarding delirium that he had not married. In reality, as he knew perfectly well, it was nothing of the kind. After he had got over Dolly, the only fever of which his somewhat cold blood had been capable was over, too, and he rose clear-eyed, as it were, to acknowledge that he was feeling a good deal more comfortable as he was. Eileen had not married, either. She looked after him excellently. They lived together with tact, sharing some but not all of their friends and going their own ways for holidays. The Turvilles were close at hand. Miss Scoby, a passionate botanist, went off every year to the flowery valleys of Switzerland while her brother motored with Cyril and Dolly in France and Italy. The arrangement had been very happy. It was strange to reflect that at one time the news that Dolly had become a widow would have made his heart jump; instead, it had remained quiet and heavy as a stone. Possibly – a painful thought – he had ended by being even more devoted to Cyril than he was to Dolly. Cyril had been such a bad painter and such a wonderfully good little human being. All of his friends had relied, almost unconsciously, on that exceptional nature – a nature for all seasons, hanging up at the back of their lives like a coat that would cherish them miraculously in any weather. None of them would know how to get on without it, Scoby least of all. As for Dolly, so often feather-brained and a trial, perhaps, even to Cyril's marvellous patience, she was a problem to which Scoby had turned his mind anxiously in the last few days. He sighed, and heard Eileen calling 'Lunch!' from the dining room. He joined her with alacrity. The melancholy morning had made him feel extremely hungry; in some strange way, the cold veal and salad and Camembert seemed to be signalling to him, Scoby, the reassuring message that he was alive.

In a few days, Dolly was back from Kent, returning with relief, almost at a run, to her bits and pieces and the familiar half of her unshared bed. When the Scobys went around to see her, they agreed later that her tiny face and figure appeared to have contracted. She sat with her bird bones tucked up in her usual chair, while they all avoided looking at the patch of hearthrug on which Cyril had had the habit of standing, rocking back and forth on the heels and toes of his ridiculous boots as he bent his serious, warm gaze down, for a change, upon some seated guest. His absence was clamorous. Getting up to play host and refill Eileen's sherry glass – the Turvilles never had spirits in the house – Scoby walked right through

the familiar spot and felt a blankness and soreness in the
heart. The miniature house, with its country air, which had
been so pretty and funny as a nest woven to the exact shape
of the perfect little Turvilles, would now obviously be
intolerable, he thought. Cyril had bought it on Scoby's advice
a few years before the war, when prices were still reasonable.
His affairs, as his friend and solicitor knew, had not been left
in such a prosperous state that Dolly would not be glad of
the excellent price it would fetch today. Cyril's generosity to
others had been too great. Scoby's mind's eye, moving more
briskly than his body, which was carefully dodging the
haunted rug on the return trip to Eileen, saw the board up
on the railings and the nest abandoned. He had already
deposited Dolly satisfactorily in a convenient flat, close, yet
not too close, to him and Eileen, by the time he sat down
again with the women.

But every death, as Scoby knew from long experience,
leaves the survivors in the boat exchanging bleak glances over
the empty place; their behaviour in the altered situation is
often unpredictable. It was really no surprise when helpless
tiny Dolly, who had left all the decisions to Cyril, now knew
with absolute certainty what she wanted. It was to continue
where she was. Perhaps because their house was the only place
in the world where Cyril's dapper form could still be said to
reside, or anyhow to have left an imprint like the warmth
lingering in a recently vacated chair, she refused to budge.
Scoby understood – he had known a pang himself at the
thought that the little place to which he and all the Turvilles'
friends had kept coming through the years would be closed to

them – yet he regarded her with the righteous exasperation of the level-headed man who sees clearly what should be done and has expected no opposition.

'Well,' he said rather abruptly, 'I suppose we'll have to make another plan.'

'Oh, Scoby, you are such a comfort,' she said, looking at him in her wheedling, loving way.

Something had remained between them through the placid years – a fondness and exact appreciation of each other's good and bad points which was almost like the tolerance of a longstanding marriage. He knew, for instance, that the understanding of money had been totally omitted from her intellectual capacity. He deplored it as one with the sight of a hawk might shake his head over a friend who has never seen the light of clear, cold, masculine day. But it was Dolly. Therefore, sighing, he began thinking what could be done.

It turned out that the rest of the Turvilles' friends were equally convinced, for their part, that they knew what she ought to do to begin life without Cyril. They were full of sensible suggestions, none of which, Scoby felt, stood a chance of being taken, however charmingly received. In the end, certain friends put their heads and their pockets together and managed to arrange things tactfully, with Scoby's help, so that Cyril's widow would not have to move out of their home. The thought upset everybody too much. They all wanted to be able to feel that something, at least, would go on. A treasured feature of their private landscapes was not to be flattened and made unrecognisable, it was felt, by a strange young man driving home along the Embankment on a moist

spring evening. The moving spirit might have gone, but they could preserve the shell. After all, as they told each other cheerfully, Dolly had few wants and should be able to manage all right. They would all make a point of dropping in from time to time to see that she was managing.

For some months, they did so with enthusiasm. Then, little by little, as cynical Scoby could have predicted would happen, they began to see less of Dolly and to have her less on their minds, too, now that they had got her safely settled in her own chair in the familiar room. Perhaps, as even Scoby had suspected of himself, Cyril was the one they had truly adored, to whom they had gone back again and again, because he gave them the sense, like a marvellously becoming mirror, of being quite as delightful and as amiable as he was while they were with him. Though such an indifferent painter, he had been a Michelangelo of friendship. And without him Dolly seemed to have been left swinging without point, like the little wooden woman figure outside a nursery weather house from which a clumsy hand has snapped off the partner whose presence made the thing work.

The Scobys, of course, were loyal, though they, too, were sadly conscious that their cheerful visits were frauds. Nothing would, nothing *could* be the same again. Eileen Scoby, a woman who could see nobody in trouble, from a cat to a whole nation, without wishing to supply nourishment in large quantities – perhaps this was why she was always most at peace in Switzerland, where everything was so visibly well nurtured that the very cows, gazing at the stocky Englishwoman with their limpid eyes, looked replete to the last, sweet blade of grass – Eileen worried conscientiously about Dolly from time to time. It seemed to her doubtful whether the little creature remembered to stock the larder or even to eat. It had been Cyril who enjoyed cooking and eating good food. Dolly was now really alarmingly frail. If Eileen had dared, she would have liked to take her a couple of chops now and then. She saw more of Dolly than Scoby did, and she noticed that Mrs Turville was becoming careless about herself in a number of small ways. A rim of ashy yellow began to lap the roots of her splendid fiery hair and was not repulsed. When Scoby's lizard eye one day noted this, too, filing away the brief, wounding fact that she had aged a great deal, his heart went through the symbolic gymnastic of smiting him. Dolly and the house appeared to be acquiring an identical air of being just slightly unkempt, which upset him, now that he had observed it. He rang her up next day and asked her to go to a concert and to supper afterward. The evening was such a success, and Dolly, by candlelight in the old favourite restaurant, looked so marvellously revived and beautiful that, reassured, he did not see her again for a month.

Some time after, when Cyril had been dead for almost a year, Eileen passed on to Scoby her suspicion that Dolly's days were punctuated by increasingly frequent trips to the sherry decanter or the wine bottle. On the telephone, she often sounded gently fuddled; sometimes she misunderstood completely what was being said to her.

'Well, if it gives her any comfort . . .' Scoby said. And if she can afford it, was the immediate footnote, added in alarm to his inward book-keeping system. How many bottles a week? He hoped not many.

'All the same, I hate the thought. Supposing she has an accident over there all by herself.'

'It's not very likely. She doesn't smoke, and there is no gas in the house, luckily.'

'It seems such a time since she went out and saw anybody except us.'

He knew that was true. Some of the old friends had practically given up inviting her, except as a matter of conscience, or inspired by a gush of affectionate memories of Cyril. The inexorable tribal laws of London were partly responsible for that. A single widow woman is difficult – so they run – to fit into an evening, and anyhow Dolly had acquired a habit of saying that she was sorry, she was doing something else. In an amazingly short time, she had dropped out of sight of everybody except the Scobys and the faithful devoted few who telephoned from time to time of an evening and heard the telephone ringing into silence.

'I know she goes to bed very early' was the formula Eileen repeated to their complaints, while her imagination saw the unpleasing vision of graceful little Dolly stretched out fast asleep, dead to the world and still fully clothed, in a house that wanted dusting and had nothing in the larder. Then she would go around and insist on taking her friend out to lunch, urging her to eat more and put on some of the lost pounds.

Soon after the anniversary of Cyril's death had passed, Scoby departed for Lebanon, where he had some business to do for a client who lived in Beirut. He enjoyed the trip. It was the first time he had been abroad since the old, happy pottering expeditions with Cyril and Dolly. Last summer, he had not felt like going off by himself, and had taken a fishing holiday with a friend. The rain had fallen relentlessly. Now, after two weeks, he flew home, the freckles darker than ever upon the sunburned skin on his crown, feeling better than he had for years. Humming cheerfully, he opened his front door as the taxi drove off down the square under the fresh, budding trees.

'Did you get my letter?' Eileen asked before he had hung up his coat.

'Letter?' He gazed at her, surprised. They were not in the habit of writing when parted, except businesslike postcards giving times of trains or planes.

'Then it must have just missed you. I knew I should have cabled.'

'Why? What has happened?' His sister's expression, he observed, was strange. He glanced round him. Their home appeared much as usual. It struck him, with a slight pre-monition of annoyance, that she had crashed their new car.

'It's Dolly. Something so extraordinary that –'

'Just a minute.' Scoby went into the hall, hung his coat in the cupboard, and returned, smiling. The buckled car had sprung back into pristine shape in his head, but the tremor had arrived in the form of a nettled sensation that he was decidedly not going to show Eileen. 'I think I can probably guess. Dolly's going to get married again.'

'How did you know?'

'Well, it wasn't very difficult, was it? She's dreadfully lonely. I must say she hasn't lost much time. Who is it?' he asked, running mentally through the short list of their unattached friends.

'She isn't going to get married. She was married last Tuesday. I was there – she did at least ask me to come. The only other person there was some man. I forget his name – a friend of Harry's.'

'I can't see why you think you ought to have cabled me, all the same,' Scoby said. The feeling of annoyance was not decreasing. 'Did you expect me to drop everything and fly back for it?'

'It's nobody we know. Harry, I mean. His name is Harry Potter. Dolly met him in that pub in the next street. I was so upset, really, that I didn't quite know what to do, except I thought you ought to know.'

Scoby looked at her blankly. 'I didn't know Dolly went to pubs.'

'She dropped in one evening, and after that she went most evenings, she said.'

Scoby was really astonished. He had nothing against pubs. They were admirable places; only the picture he suddenly had of diminutive Dolly, a woman of her age and tastes, sitting in a corner sipping her sherry in the haze of smoke and squash of drinking bodies, was a ludicrous one. Why couldn't she do her little tippling in the home that her friends' fondness had made secure for her? He tried to think of her as a 'regular', exchanging jokes with the customers. And at the same time he knew the answer. He had just supplied it himself. She had been wretchedly lonely. All the annoyance was with himself and Eileen, that they had not been able to do better by her, and, obliquely, by Cyril, than that. 'Why didn't you go and see her more?' he burst out, most unfairly.

'I saw her all I could. One can't always be there.'

'I know, I know.' Scoby smiled appeasingly at his sister, whose face had flushed up quickly, as though his words had hit her painfully across it. 'I think she might have waited until I got back,' he said merely.

'Well, of course, but if you ask me, I'm sure she felt it was a good plan to rush everything through while you were away.'

'Why, for God's sake? One could hardly stop her doing anything she wanted to do. But it would have been friendlier, considering everything. I only hope it's all right.' Belatedly, his imagination groped toward his irreplaceable friend's successor. 'Who is Potter?'

'He has one of those little antique shops off the King's Road. He used to live over it, but now he has moved in with Dolly. She says they're going to run the shop together.'

'Well, that might be a good idea,' Scoby said. 'Dolly was always good at that sort of thing.'

'He's younger than she by quite a bit, I should say. Dolly says they're the same age, but I doubt it. He's been married before, but his wife went off with someone. If Dolly hadn't told me that, I wouldn't really have thought he was the marrying type.'

Scoby gave a short exasperated laugh. He was suddenly conscious of having made a long journey and of wanting a bath. How like Dolly, he thought, to arrange things so that her

affairs would descend upon him, like a practical-joke device suspended over his front door, the moment he got home. 'Does everyone else know?' he asked. He named two or three of the Turvilles' most faithful friends.

'I don't know. They may, by now. Oh!' Eileen burst out. 'What I don't understand is, how could she, after Cyril?'

'What is he really like?' Scoby could not help feeling very curious.

His sister hesitated. Then she smiled. 'You can see for yourself, tomorrow. Dolly has asked us to have a drink.'

Harry Potter himself opened the front door the following evening. Scoby had come from his office, and Eileen had already arrived. The lawyer saw before him a tall, shambling man, dressed in tweeds and what Scoby noted as an unspeakable shirt. This stranger, after advancing a loose-feeling assortment of fingers, ushered Scoby into the room he knew as well as his own. The evening had turned chilly. A little fire crackled pleasantly in the grate, before which Eileen stood on Cyril's bit of hearthrug, a glass in her hand. Dolly sprang up from her chair to stand on tiptoe and pull Scoby's head down toward her.

'Well, Dolly, you've given all your friends a surprise,' he said, kissing her warmly. Over her head – newly flaming as though fresh from the hairdresser, he observed immediately – he exchanged glances briefly with Eileen.

Dolly smiled up at him a little uncertainly. 'It didn't seem right without you there, Scoby. But it all happened so suddenly, didn't it, Harry?'

'When Dolly made up her mind, I didn't want to give her a minute's chance to change it again,' said the bridegroom, showing a number of tobacco-stained teeth. He made this statement with great simplicity. Turning to Scoby, who was eyeing him curiously, he asked, 'Whisky, or would you rather have a gin?'

'Whisky, thanks.' The days of sherry were evidently over.

Potter crossed the floor, which quaked beneath his tread, and busied himself at – Scoby could not help feeling with stupid resentment – Cyril's drinks table.

'How brown you are!' Dolly cried, putting her arm through Scoby's. Joining Eileen, they all three stood on top of Cyril. Scoby thought, not unpleased, that only he had remembered. He raised the large drink that Potter put into his hand and said, 'Here's to you both.'

After the first swallow, he looked at Potter again, as though the taste might have changed his first impression, which had been one of quite ludicrous astonishment. It had been caused by the merely physical, of course. It was ridiculous that he should not have expected Dolly to be drawn to someone as unlike Cyril as he could possibly be. The effect of Potter in the Turvilles' dim, precious little room was that of a Gulliver captured, hauled in, and tacked down by who knows what invisible threads on the miniature sofa, which had been scaled to Cyril's legs. It was so low for its present occupant that he had evident difficulty, after seating himself upon it, in juggling with his glass and the silver snuffbox, containing cigarettes, which he brought out of his pocket and offered Scoby. He avoided his own knees and managed everything finally with a sort of slow precision. He wore dark glasses, perhaps because of some affliction of the eyes, and this gave his face a certain anonymous quality that Scoby found disconcerting. The areas of flesh surrounding these circles of defensive blackness looked pallid, fleshy, and amiable. There was something soft and somewhat feminine about him; it explained Eileen's hesitation. He had a good nose, which had survived the surrounding wreckage, as noses do. But he looked a bit seedy, a bit bashed about by life, perhaps. Scoby had had an awful fear that Eileen's description might have been too restrained, and that he would find that poor Dolly had married some odd fish who was young enough to be her son. Younger than she he certainly was, but Scoby could not decide by how much.

'Are you and Dolly going to stay on here?' Scoby asked while Dolly and Eileen were talking.

'Yes, I think so. It's handy for the shop, for one thing, and it couldn't be more delightful. I love it. It has wonderful atmosphere. And it's perfect for her, don't you think?' He glanced over at Dolly, who was looking, Scoby had to admit to himself, a new woman – by which he meant that she was really looking the old Dolly, the real and original Dolly who for more than a year had vanished from her friends' sight.

'We all thought so,' Scoby said shortly, speaking for the Turvilles' dear, bereaved friends who had come here for so many years as though to some little shrine off the beaten track of the world, where they knew something better than themselves existed. What had happened to them all? He stared into his glass.

'We met at the local, you know. She was always alone, so one evening I asked her to have a drink. After that, we found we had a lot in common. You knew Mr Turville well, didn't you?'

'We were very old friends.'

'I wish I had known him. Dolly has told me so much about him that I feel I do, almost. He must have been a wonderful character. How do you think that looks, by the way?' He nodded toward the fireplace, and Scoby saw what he would have noticed directly he came in if he had not been so absorbed in looking Potter over. Ever since he could remember, a cloudy oval gilt-framed mirror, holding out sconces for candles, had hung there, but now it had been replaced by one of Cyril's series of 'Dolly' portraits – was it 'Dolly 10' or 'Dolly 13'? Like Potter, it was far too big for the room. Dressed in a Chinese coat, pretty as Cyril's horribly sweet paint could make her, and indecently young, Dolly looked down with a teasing smile at the three middle-aged whisky-drinking strangers – four, Scoby might have said, except that Potter's age was a poser. He was a no man's land to Scoby, accustomed as he was to dealing with men of certain accents, incomes, and attitudes. Cyril, too, had been an exception, but that was different.

Scoby glanced quickly at Dolly. She was telling Eileen some story, with a great deal of laughter and gesturing of her small hands, and he reflected that whisky was not her usual drink. He said, 'I didn't greatly admire Cyril's work, to be truthful. It's a pleasant picture, of course.'

'He's completely out of fashion now, certainly. Dolly thinks he'll come into his own one day, and I'm sure she's right. I love it. It's a beautiful thing, and so like Dolly now. I persuaded her to let me hang it, and we think it would be nice to change it every now and then for another of the "Dolly" series.'

Scoby gave him an impenetrable lizard stare. He had begun to feel that Dolly had indeed hooked a very odd fish, but at the same time he was amused. Potter spoke with the unctuous solemnity of a guardian showing someone round a sacred place. With his big, dark glasses and his big, soft face, he looked owlish, and also, in those hairy brown tweeds, like a rather nice, shabby dog. Scoby trusted that his host's knowledge of antiques was sounder than his taste in art. Surrendering his empty glass to Potter, he looked round him and noticed that the room had changed in other respects. Like Dolly, it had a great air of being renewed and garnished. Someone had polished it until it shone – he smelled the pleasant smell of the wax – and he could only think that Potter was the proud housewife. He could imagine the man, an apron round his middle, diligently scrubbing and brushing – even taking a needle and thread to Dolly, who, in the last year, had acquired such a sad, uncaring air of coming apart.

Scoby had begun the visit feeling nervous and strained, but before long he began to feel relaxed. It was hard to say why, but something pleasant was in the air besides the smell of furniture polish. It had been a tiring day, but he sat on. He had half a mind to accept the invitation given presently to stay for supper.

'I'm a good cook,' said Potter encouragingly.

'No, we must go,' said Scoby, glancing at Eileen.

'Another evening soon, then,' Dolly said.

Scoby was sitting beside her now, on the sofa. Potter got up to show Eileen the beauties of a bit of furniture across the room. He was talking vehemently. He's really not too bad, thought Scoby.

Dolly leaned forward suddenly. 'What do you think of him?' she murmured. She added immediately, 'Don't say, because it doesn't matter. Do you know why I married him? You must have been surprised. It's because he's so like Cyril.'

With difficulty, Scoby restrained a bark of laughter. The thought of his lost friend was comically at odds with the flesh and blood before him of the loose-limbed antique dealer, who had just lifted Dolly's table in his large hands as though it were a walnut, the better to show a detail to Eileen. He gazed at his dear, idiotic Dolly with a blend of fondness and irritation. She was incapable of recognising the irreplaceable. 'We must go,' he said more loudly to Eileen's back.

Potter stopped Scoby for a moment or two while the women went toward the door, so that he could expound all over again on the charms of the table. 'Dolly bought it for three pounds in Colchester before the war,' he said. 'She has a really marvellous eye. I always trust her taste.' He set down the table delicately, took off his dark glasses, and briefly mopped his eyes with a handkerchief. Then, without replacing the goggles, he looked at Scoby. 'It was one of the interests that brought us together, of course,' he said.

Scoby muttered something. Potter's exposed eyes were weak – a washed-out hazel colour – but there was no mistaking their expression. It was startlingly that of Cyril's unforgettable blue ones. Scoby had the uncanny impression that his friend was beaming gently down at him from that pudgy face. The recognition was instantaneous. Shaken, he hastened after the women, made his farewells, and followed Eileen down the front steps. As they crossed the road, he looked back. It was twilight. Potter was still standing, an arm dropped round Dolly's shoulders, the two of them outlined in the lighted doorway.

They went inside, and the door shut. Scoby could imagine Potter carefully locking up. The little shrine was closed for the day. Yet he had a feeling that now the circle of deserting Turville regulars would return, at first out of curiosity when they heard the news, and then because of something else which he could not quite define. Yes, as their helpless Dolly had done so unerringly, he reflected, they would recognise what they had missed, all of them, since Cyril's death. And unable for once to file his thoughts neatly, for the mixture of relief on Dolly's behalf and faint melancholy on his own was confusing, he said little as he and Eileen walked home, only agreeing with his sister's suddenly cheerful conviction that, after all, everything had happened for the best.

If you have enjoyed this Persephone book why not telephone or write to us for a free copy of the Persephone Catalogue and the current Persephone Biannually? All Persephone books ordered from us cost £13 or three for £33 plus £2.50 postage per book.

PERSEPHONE BOOKS LTD
59 Lamb's Conduit Street
London WC1N 3NB

Telephone: 020 7242 9292
sales@persephonebooks.co.uk
www.persephonebooks.co.uk